CW00339883

BARE
LIT

edited by

kavita bhanot
courttia newland
mend mariwany

brain mill press
green bay, wisconsin

Published in the United States by Brain Mill Press.
Print ISBN 978-1-942083-58-0
EPUB ISBN 978-1-942083-60-3
MOBI ISBN 978-1-942083-59-7
PDF ISBN 978-1-942083-61-0

www.brainmillpress.com

contents

Literature by writers of colour published in the UK remains overburdened by a bulk of constraints. Often it fixes complicated narratives to personal struggles, consigning them to domains of the confessionnal, inner moral clashes, and the impossibly tragic.

The inauguration of the Bare Lit Festival in February 2016 marked a significant turning point. Rather than centring writers' work around prescriptive themes, the festival looked to open possibilities beyond them. Through readings, conversations, panels, and performances, we were adamant to overcome the anachronism that exists between the vast spectrum of work produced by writers of colour and the kind of exposure they receive. With the generous help of our audiences and supporters, Bare Lit was able to honour their work both artistically and financially.

The accompanying anthology builds upon this achievement. Calling on participants and writers of colour UK-wide, we asked contributors to submit their writing in line with the aims and ethos of Bare Lit. The response was overwhelming—thank you to everyone who contributed.

We received over a hundred submissions of prose and poetry covering an impressive range. Writers took us on flights of fancy, pandering to multiple worlds while engaging us in their literary imaginations. Every submission was carefully discussed and considered on the premise of originality, relevance, and often a certain kind of gut feeling.

bare lit anthology

The selection presented here brings together original, previously unpublished works of contemporary prose and poetry by established as well as lesser known writers, giving both the opportunity to work with this volume's brilliant editors, Kavita Bhanot and Courttia Newland, who have honed each piece to its utmost and without whom the anthology would not have been possible. The final pieces cover an unimaginably vast scope, reflecting the wide, and at times irreconcilable and contradictory, range of themes and the political élan present in the work of writers of colour in this particular period. In this sense, they are not canonical but anticanonical, and vested in the many global and diasporic vernaculars.

The Bare Lit 2016 anthology has captured the animate spirit of our festival, which for so many of our writers and readers has signalled a growing and unwavering confidence amongst writers of colour in the British literary landscape. It builds upon a long-lasting and important tradition of defiant literary collectives and volumes by British Caribbean, African, and Asian diaspora writers who have worked so diligently to carve out spaces for conversations.

Putting together this volume, however, was a question of balancing texts, choosing between those evoking a political consciousness and those driven by a desire to explore themes and styles in their own, perhaps more unassuming, way. Making selections for an anthology is never easy, and no collection is ever exhaustive or complete. As editors and publishers we understand how politicised the role of selection, of representing the right kinds of texts, is. Through commitment and continual discussions we agreed to include a wide-as-possible spectrum in equal measures and offer a nuanced view of what is present and what needs to be more present.

Whether intentional or accidental, the stories and poetry are unsettling to the white literary establishment— not because they dismantle but because their sheer scope undermines the monolithic imagery surrounding writers of colour. Their variety reminds us of the possible and potential variables that exist in our prismatic lives. It's for that reason that our choices do not reflect only the quality of works submitted to us, but also our own political intentions and ambitions as editors. By choosing some work over others we wanted to avoid oversaturating the literary landscape with texts of a certain kind.

And so the selection presented compiles a handful of texts by participating writers from our festival in 2016 and complements them with texts from writers who weren't present but responded to our call for submissions. We have featured some of the most promising texts. They pander to the historical over the allegorical, to more personal meditations, and span a plethora of literary styles and genres. While some explore the intersections of identity, race, gender, and class, others are textured by introspective voyages. Some are unprecedented in the themes they address; others offer sharp takes on more familiar ones. In fact, the narratives escape our impulse to assume any real categorization.

The pieces we've put together take us from the Caribbean over the Indian subcontinent to the UK to fictitious, perhaps visionary, places, but most importantly they remind us that writers of colour are not tied to the inscriptions of the publishing industry. In spite of the challenges faced, they can free themselves of the constraints placed upon them if they have the space to do so. With this anthology we hope to offer our own contribution and pay homage to such efforts.

We are extremely proud to present this exciting collection. And while this is the first Bare Lit anthology, we look forward to contributing to and collaborating with existing and emerging platforms in the future.

Mend Mariwany
Co-Founder of Bare Lit
Co-Editor, *Bare Lit* anthology

introduction

kavita bhanot and courttia newland

We have seen, post Brexit and Donald Trump's election, a fresh turn towards literature—as if, in these 'barbaric' times, the 'civilised' sphere of literature offers some sanity, that it might save us. But is it true that literature, in itself, offers an alternative to the racism and white supremacy that manifests so clearly today? Does literature, in its essence, challenge the idea of the 'other'? Or has literature always played a part in the 'othering' that is at the heart of such racism and supremacy—perhaps all the more dangerous as it is not seen or recognized, partly due to the pervasive belief that reading and writing literature makes us better people?

From the work of Edward Said to Toni Morrison to Ngugi Wa thiong'o, from Chinua Achebe's critique of Conrad's *Heart of Darkness* to Hamid Debashi's *Brown Skin White Masks*, it has been made clear that literature perpetuates and normalizes racist stereotypes, prejudice. So why does this mythologizing of literature persist? Why are we so reluctant to take 'literature' off its pedestal, to face up to the fact that literature can be and has been a site for normalized oppressions and supremacies, including whiteness? That literature is political. It does not—as Lionel Shriver seemed to assume in her recent speech at Brisbane Writers Festival critiquing 'political correctness' and calling for the writer's right to freedom of expression—occupy a sacred sphere, separate from the world. And we don't, writing into this abstract space, write simply for ourselves or for no-one in particular, as so many writers continue to insist. Rather, much of the English language literature that we read and write tends, consciously or unconsciously, to be directed towards white readers as the invisible, dominant, normative perspective.

The shared understanding that literature is entangled in the world, not separate and superior from it—that literature always faces in a specific direction—has been our starting point in putting together this collection, the first of an annual series published by Media Diversified, the Bare Lit Festival, and Brain Mill Press. It has been an honour for us to have been invited to edit this anthology. It has been a relief, in the process of putting it together, not to have to hide or suppress our understanding of literature as political. It has felt like the lifting of a common yet unspoken censorship, to have conversations around what we would like to include in the anthology that are not simply based on 'merit'—on some narrowly defined but apparently universal ideas of craft, of 'good' literature—but to consider also the ways in which a piece represents, who it is directed towards, the risks it takes, the emotion and honesty behind it (recognizing the politics of both).

We have been surprised and delighted by so many of our submissions, and are proud of what this anthology brings together. At the heart of this project has been an effort to address directly the suppression of the voice of the writer of colour in mainstream literature—a silencing that is rarely addressed via essays, articles, or novels and stories, even today. Few writers of colour have dared to tackle the very real ways in which literature can become something of a performance, where the frameworks of how we should write are often fixed, defined outside of ourselves, with very little room for maneuver. Hardly any emphasis is placed on the monocultural nature of published literature, save the odd periodic report such as Writing the Future; thus, we are offered few creative examples of how to extend ourselves beyond the parameters of what we already see. Instead, the blame is laid at the feet of the writers; we're routinely told that we don't make enough money, or we're not writing well enough. This is not the case. Working with writers as we do, in universities, via literary consultancies, as editors and award judges, we're privy to a great deal of writing that often doesn't make it to the shelves. Our literature is as rich, broadly defined, and imaginative as any other. It's the assumptions of an industry that deems the marketplace less sophisticated than it actually is that holds writers back.

As we see in this collection, writers are doing the necessary work. Away from the demands of marketing departments, they sit at their desks experimenting with language and form. They engage with the politics of the moment and the spirit of their emotions, in an attempt to gain a greater understanding of who we are. They wrestle with their chosen art, be it fiction, or poetry or theatre, or film, and they make the work they wish to see. It's an enormously brave and often unrewarding act.

As editors, we wanted to make a space that allowed the existence of such work, and by doing so, allowed the existence of us. In our call out, we encouraged writers of colour to send in work that challenged the inherited frameworks into which we are supposed to fit ourselves and our writing, work that dared to venture into the unsaid and unexplored, work that they thought they would have difficulty getting published elsewhere. In some way, all the pieces in this anthology—poems, short stories, and the pieces that fit neither category—transcend these boundaries of what we are supposed to write, of what is acceptable, palatable, marketable.

At the same time, we don't make any claims for this anthology as groundbreaking—it is an important step in the direction that we need to go, part of a necessary process in which we create safe, nurturing, mutually supportive spaces for our art, for seeing and exploring realities, experiences, imaginative journeys that the structures around us actively prevent us from seeing and exploring. We hope that Bare Lit Festival along with this first *Bare Lit* anthology represent the beginning of this process.

postscript from the black atlantic
koye oyedeji

1. IT DIDN'T SEEM TO MATTER THAT THE FIRST GIRL WENT MISSING WHILE HE WAS STILL AT SEA.

It was going to take two weeks for the ocean liner to reach the United Kingdom, but Lawal hoped that the journey—the time between worlds—would help bridge the divide between homeland and sanctuary, shame and prosperity. He was young, but there was already much to put behind him and so, by day, as the ship sailed aside the coast of west Africa, he let his optimism ride along, surfing the slate-grey waves his ancestors once worshipped. But even the ancestors can grow impatient, and, once the liner crossed into European waters, the waves began to blacken at night and throw their strength at the ship's hull. When this did no good (or bad), the ancestors grew enraged, and they began to tell of the way in which this young man and his family name had insulted the rivers and forgotten that it was the mother of the ocean who had given them their blessings. They sent the waves a little something to help them along, unwrapping a curse as thick as the fog that would descend on the maritime mornings. Lawal was none the wiser though, wrapped up in things unseen—his travels and his ambition, a sense of spirit that stirred within and flooded his arteries with the promise of something; a tingle that felt like fortune, an air that trapped his lungs with the swallow of success.

But he spent a lot of time on the deck; perhaps too long, because it was as if the wind began to carry his confidence away. He had enough time alone now, alone with his thoughts for the first time in weeks. He recalled the ways in which he tried to conceal the house girl's stomach and, when he knew he no longer could, the way his father had looked at him when he told him the news. His father had beat him, but then immediately called for the house girl and beat her even harder. He recalled how she remained silent through it all, and how her silence just angered his father even more. And he believed that it was the silence that was beginning to haunt him now. After a week of rough weather, storms, and fierce winds, he stopped going onto the deck altogether, returning only when the isles came into view, when the rush and adrenaline of the other passengers swept him up top. Seeing the smog of Liverpool on the horizon, he fancied himself as some sort of cosmic revisionist, using the present moment—and all sense of accomplishment it brought—to disabuse himself of any past wrongs. He had sacrificed the comfort of home. But he could be a part of this alien community; fresh produce in the Mother country—a land both strange and familiar. He'd made it to England in one piece despite it feeling for a time as though God had personally sent them the worst of his weather. And now that he had arrived, Lawal believed he would move past the detritus that his lust and longing had left in their wake. He was going to make his father proud; he was going to seal the fissures he had created and discard the past as though it were merely old clothes.

But the ancestors were talking. And he was talking over them with all of these thoughts—thought after thought after thought. If he had stopped for silence, he might've heard something rippling, his evil catching up with him, slow crawling across the ocean beneath him.

2. HE THOUGHT THAT THEY WOULD COME TO LOVE HIM IN TIME...

...But Liverpool was no good to him. He was never allowed to settle. Never allowed to feel as if he might belong. He spent a year there before he left for London, where he was able to find a decaying slice of low-rent council housing—a flat on a block that was barely holding court on a crumbling estate. London was no better for him, but he thought the city might give him what Liverpool could not, that opportunity loomed in the shadows of its tall buildings, beneath the bellows of the market traders and in the churning inflections of the lecturers at the Polytechnic he attended. Two years of nothing passed, and until success came out from behind its rock, he had to content himself with thoughts of home and the thought of what had become home. Piss stains crawled down the stairwells in his building and the walls were spray painted with British National Party slogans, calling cards that demanded, "WOGS GO HOME."

Still, despite all the fetor, there was a different stink in the air. Lucy Smalls, a quiet nine-year-old brunette, had not been seen in over a month. She was the youngest of three girls, raised by the single mother who lived on the east side of Lawal's building, in flat 38. Natasha Ifill, who had lived with her family just a few doors away from him, had been close to Lucy's age when, two years ago, she had also disappeared. And just as in the case of Natasha, the pieces of sticky tape that held the missing posters to the buildings' walls would come away in time, and the posters would begin to tell a different story, to peel, tear, and flap with the wind. No one in the community made it their task to repair or replace Natasha's posters; they waited instead and, flush with the guilt of still being able to hug their own children, they relied on the elements to discard their fears.

This piece of south London, with all the police presence, the unease and the anxiety, was Lawal's home and would remain so until, in some fashion, he was able to make a distant father proud. The months tumbled one after another in a place like that; long-term plans easily unraveled.

Snap your fingers. He was now a grown man. His twenties behind him, but still no better for wear. Still living between strangers. Still the city continued to greet him with forced smiles and spurious expressions of welcome. London was impatient with his English and his pronunciations, unsympathetic when it came to late rent. Each day he rediscovered the shade of his skin. He grew accustomed to the words that were frequently spun in his direction. A familiar crop of slurs—Nigger. Golliwog. Sambo. He would ignore the insults until he got home, where, once sat at the kitchen table, his head in his hands, he would peel the words apart and try to reassemble them with his own understanding. The cold UK air was potent, and the winters were unforgiving. Who could have told him that the frequent rain would be able to wash the colour from his ambition, or that January's snow could cause his confidence to ebb away?

So it was quite causal, then, that during one of those brutal winters, he found God waiting for him, in the form of a south London Pentecostal church that was giving away free food with season's greetings.

3. GOD MAY OR MAY NOT HAVE BEEN BY HIS SIDE

He was rummaging in his pocket for his keys when the four men encountered him. They were like clones, impulsive and united by their fear of invasion. Their heads were shaved and they dressed alike in bomber jackets, their fatigue trousers tucked into the top of their Doc Marten boots. Their danger was in their number. Because if they were not four, then they might not have taken him by each appendage, and the violence—the idea of picking him up and tossing him over the balcony—might not have come so easy to them.

Lawal fell three floors from the block of flats just as

something unseen quickened itself and chased his descent. He hit the pathway outside the garages and lay on the spalled concrete until he was able to comprehend his consciousness. He still lived. He barely caught his breath before he realised his fortune. There wasn't even any blood to speak of. *A miracle?* he thought, before he climbed to his feet and winced at the pain in his back and the sudden headache that rang between his ears, the early murmurs of a dull throb that would never subside, welcoming in a pain he was going to spend the rest of his long life trying to shake loose. He shuffled back towards the building then, unsteadied, still trying to gather the world beneath his feet. But later, when his shock set him free, and the fear set in that with so many different Gods in the world he might snub whatever higher being had come to his aid, he heard the first two of what would be many voices. Two voices in his head. Two girls that screamed and pleaded with him to stop.

4. IT WAS GOING TO BE A BURDEN TOO MUCH TO BEAR.

And then those two young girls disappeared. He'd read it in the paper as Jide, one of his few friends from the Pentecostal church, fussed over him, bent on reminding him that their God was a jealous God and that he needed to stop all this recent talk of embracing all faiths, of Ifa and Islam, Hinduism and Buddhism. At church, Lawal had a growing reputation as he began to insist that they evenly spread their praise amongst the gods, to not forget the names of Allah and Brahman and Oludumare in their whispers. Members of the congregation had be-

gun to share their concerns with Jide. They found Lawal's words inappropriate, and it was distasteful of him
to attend each service in the same pair of dirty jeans.
Talk amongst the church members grew. Brother Lawal
was practicing *juju*, he was bringing evil spirits into their
house of God. The pastor spoke to Lawal a handful of
times, but when it grew clear that his message had fall-
en on deaf ears Lawal was asked not to return. He quit
his graduate studies soon after this and lost the job he
held as a night watchman at a paper factory. The voices he heard made it difficult for him to work or study
and, fearing another attack, he rarely ever went outside,
leaving the flat only to visit the post office to cash his
unemployment benefit or to the market to buy gari and
yams. The rent arrears piled up. Jide stopped visiting.
Lawal would talk, instead, to strangers because he found
that when he talked the voices dimmed a little. But it
didn't take much of this before people started to cross
the street whenever they encountered him. That's how
he began to talk to the kids. Because the kids were yet to
form judgments and prejudices—the only people innocent enough to give him their time.

5. THEY WERE VOICES CLOTHED IN GLOOM.

Snap your fingers again and, just like that, two, six, eight
voices were now in their hundreds. Conversation was his
only palliative; he was only able to speak over the voices
when he had someone to speak to. It was as though he'd
taken up the task of carrying the souls of the locals, and

it was better for him to talk than to cave beneath the weight of their thoughts.

And so he talked.

His willingness to talk to anyone, to strangers and to the children, meant he earned some local names. Nothing very clever. The Nigerian. The Voodoo Man. The Nigerian Voodoo Man. The Witchdoctor. He ignored the jeers and once managed to just avoid the brick a teenager hurled at him. But when the skinheads chased him a second time he decided that being social was not for him. He shut the world out. More importantly, perhaps, he shut his landlord out. He scrawled stuff about his home, transcriptions of the quickened voices that whispered beneath his every act. It helped, not as much as talking did, but it numbed him somewhat. On his refrigerator, in black permanent marker, he put down everything he heard, like the thoughts of the A-Level student who was sure she knew better than her teacher, and the skinhead boy who didn't share the same views his friends had on Jews and blacks but envied how having a collective voice came so easy to them. He heard the agony of the longtime married woman, a long time untouched. He heard the anxious father infuriated by his son's shrug.

Soon, everywhere he looked in his home, he saw sentence after sentence, written wherever there was a clean surface to be found—on plug sockets, on tables, on the skirting, all over the bath. From his perch on the windowsill, he looked out amongst the flats, he saw us—you, me—for what we really were, lead actors in our stories, marked by our inability to shed our sense

of significance. But it was those close to him, his neighbours—his community—whose thoughts seeped in with
the most intensity. He heard the bigotry, the addiction to
alcohol, the protectiveness, the settling for second best,
the lust, the trepidation to look at your own body in the
mirror and, within it all, he heard the thoughts of *that*
man—the driven, impulsive man who lingered with the
young girls—as well as the torment of those who had
lost a daughter, granddaughter, and sister to this man.
Lawal thought the voices were all so violent; it seemed
as if violence was everywhere, and the more he heard it,
the more it sickened him, suffocating the optimism he'd
stockpiled during his earlier years in the country.

He had been prepared. He knew that like any good
religion his faith would waver, that it would dull and that
he would be desensitised to its effects, just like the lingering pain in his head. And he realised there was no
chasing the past, and the future was unattainable. The
ambition he had in the seventies had given way to the
resignation the eighties brought, and there was only the
now, and the time to make peace with something—some
being that had chased him across the waters. For the
first time in a long time, he thought of the bastard child,
born out of wedlock, who his father had hurried him
away from. The child would be a teenager now, away
from the big city of Lagos, living in whatever village her
mother's family was from. And for the first time ever,
he thought of the child's mother, the untrained and unkempt fourteen-year-old house girl they had taken on.
And he confessed aloud, for the first time, that she was
not for him to use as his own. She was not another item

of furniture in their large home. He confessed aloud, for the first time, that she was no seductress; that he had dragged her to the Boys' Quarters where he raped her, and that he had done so several times.

And an affirmation came with the confession—that the past's denials and the haunting thoughts of the present had something in common: they were voices clothed in gloom.

6. WHEN THEY FOUND HIM, THEY FOUND THEIR ASSURANCE...

...But not before the eight-year-old Pakistani girl, Fatima Bachani, went missing. Her parents didn't understand English. But no vernacular would help them understand what had happened. They were inconsolable. Lost to the world as much as their child was. Lawal could've been right there with Fatima when she was lifted off the monkey bars in the play area. He'd felt her uncertainty, her confusion, and later her fear. His faith completely withered after that, the voices grew in volume, and he grew as accustomed to living with them as he did with the headache. He would hear voices over and over wherever he went. There were so many voices now that they talked over one another, and he could no longer make out what was being said. The din became just another soundtrack to his life, just a portion of the gloom he felt. There was nothing to do then but to consider the voices as both a warning for others and punishment to him. He force-fed himself some faith and decided that fasting might help—a marathon fast of Jesus-like proportions. He would fast for forty days for the lives of others and for his own salvation—or he would die trying. And so he stopped eating, stopped collecting his unemployment benefit, and would never have left his home again under his own volition.

Being a tenant in an illegally sublet home bought him time; not even his landlord was able to act without alerting the council. But his life, as with all lives, was a blur that brushes the blur of others, and the authorities broke in on the seventh day, after the water he left slowly running in the bathroom sink overflowed to a point where it began to drip into the flat below. In the unkempt and now flooded home, they found him in the barely furnished bedroom. Karma had done a number on him. He was lying on a mattress, naked and emaciated, whispering prayers as he lay in his waste, his urine, and his faeces—selflessly praying for all of us amongst all that mess...

On the wall above him there was a postscript from the Black Atlantic; barely legible and written in excrement stood the words: *I raped her.*

It was the one sentence he felt he could hold on to through the orchestra of noise, and he muttered this over and over again as one police officer retched and another radioed for an ambulance.

7. NO ONE CAN EXONERATE THE FORGOTTEN.

He would bounce from one institution to another.

The detective inspector working the investigation closed the book on the case of the missing girls.

And it was never opened again.

Not even when, weeks later, Greta's daughter disappeared.

Instead, a new chapter was written.

selina nwulu

We're not hiring any black girls this season too much sass. bad attitude. jezebel. ink blot. too much chunk. ratchet. coming for you. too much **They just don't have the right aesthetic.** too much spice. thick lip. nappy knot. ink blot stain. baartman bounce. suffocating you. too much. **We're following what sells.** too much temptress. jungle fever bite. crotch creep. silent shudder. wet. too much bruise. an ink blot spoiling the clothes. too much. **We're going for a very specific look.** too much choke. rage. hip jut. grit. overspill. cheap sell. spoiling the clothes. an ink blot spoiling the clothes. too much **European. These girls tend to have fewer curves.** Keep it Simple Keep it Straight Whip Straight Flowing Keep it Clean Uniform Pure Keep it Clear Understood Keep it Chic Keep it Current Keep it Picture Perfect Keep it Now. Keep it.

selina nwulu

Don't translate/
my beauty is a language
you do not know how to speak

till all that's left is white space

selina nwulu

I found my body parts at the
bottom of an editor's bin
loose rinds of the lips
my mother gave me
a yanked tooth
the bridge of my brow
wilted laugh lines
shredded coils of hair
the scrunched petals of my nose
fistfuls of plump
shades of my skin
seeping out of the sides
until there was light, so much light
and I think:
this is an angelic death, isn't it?
a slow smother
an obsessive throttle
a constant murder

blue cornflowers

salena godden

S he stands behind the bar and sings to herself:
Bring me the used and abused, the battered and bruised, your scars I will follow like train tracks, your clothes as rough as potato sacks. She sings, bring me the broken and the battered, with his wounded heart worn on his frayed sleeve. Bring me the tarnished tin soldiers, the cowboys that cry, the washed-up pirates. Bring me the broken-nosed boxer who says he could have been a contender. Bring me the patient and never the doctor. Bring me the convict, not the lawyer and never the judge. Bring me the worn out, the worked over and the worked through, the win nothing and the lost it all. She sings, bring me the half full and never the half empty.

Fresh out of prison, he goes into The Crown, his first pint on the outside, he spots her a mile off. She works behind the bar and she's just his type, she wants to save the world one man at a time. She's a tough bird with a big heart of gold, he says, she's a bit mad, but she's got spirit. He boasts, if you get your feet under her table, you'll be looked after, alright, you'll be well fed and watered, she'll even do you a fry-up and give you money, the morning after, for your bus home. Bless her.

I don't know how she does it, night after night, that stinking pub, all those drunks and hard knocks, but she still looks for the good in people, she sees the gold in people. And the worst part is, she thinks she's the one doing the saving. She wants to be a knight in shining armour, funny that, isn't it, because right now she's the one that needs saving most, she's the one that could use someone being decent for once, and now isn't that the truth.

She says that life is not about how you fall, it's how you get up, time and time again, its about how you get up. And what don't kill you, will only make you stronger, my love, what don't kill you, only makes you stronger. So she gives everyone a chance and a second chance. And she says you're welcome, come again, just remember to wipe your feet and use a coaster for your glass of beer. But the truth is, she shows you her hand, she plays life so open, it is impossible not to see her cards, to cheat her and beat her.

She wakes up in his strange bed. He sleeps and snores gently. She turns her head and sees his shaved head, the top of his arm out of the covers, his botched blue prison tattoos on his bicep. She gets up, careful not to wake him, and walks to the window and pulls the nylon net curtains aside. Outside she sees the industrial estate, as grey as a pint glass of old dishwater. Pissing it down, just as you would expect in July in Belfast.

I'll look back on this, one day, she thinks, and I'll wonder what the hell I was doing here. I didn't just let go of the kite. My kite isn't just knotted in the tree. Oh no, I snapped the kite string, I jumped off the roof of the world with my kite rope tied to a rock, sinking into this black and bottomless lake of trouble. I lost the map and stopped paying attention. I'll keep trucking on in spite of everything, even though I know I am in the wrong place, I know this road will go somewhere. All roads lead somewhere, eventually, don't they?

She looks at his cluttered floor, then over at the table, a jumble of mugs and beer cans, a debris of crumpled and ripped Rizla packets and several full ashtrays. She catches her reflection in the mirror, sighs and says, Jeremy Kyle.

This makes her chuckle and think of a one-hundred-and-forty-character joke but she won't tweet it. She's wearing his old T-shirt, her big tits bounce and ache, she is pale faced and milky. Today she promises herself she must go to the doctors. She has to get tested, get this sorted. She knows she is not right. She swigs tepid tap water out of a tea-stained mug and waits to stop feeling nauseous.

Then she gives up the morning and climbs back into his warm bed. She moves her hand down his firm body, strokes the black hairs of his belly, he murmurs sleepily. She strokes his hot balls and feels him get hard, he rolls onto his back and stretches. His eyes closed, his breath-

ing deep. Soon he begins to moan, she touches him,
kisses his throat, his neck, his shoulder. She can work
two hands, two hands at the same time, one on his fat
dick and one on herself. Wet with last night's come and
now a new wetness. She moves down the bed and sucks
his cock. He wakes up to feed her and fuck her mouth.
He grips her hair, pushes his fat cock into her mouth.
She is writhing, bucking, jolting, quickly, she is coming,
on her own fingers, she is coming now, and he climbs
on top of her and is in her and he is fucking her and he
is coming, coming on her, coming in her and with her.
The damage is already done. She hides her face in his
shoulder and neck and cries silently and quickly thinks,
this is the last time, she thinks, this is over.

She did ask him if he would come to England with
her, and he said he probably shouldn't or wouldn't or
couldn't, she cannot quite remember which, but he isn't
coming. She didn't ask twice, she wanted him to insist,
to be a man about it, to look her in the eye and to hold
her and say,

'Everything will be alright my girl, you'll not go
through this alone…'

But he said nothing and she could tell he'd rather not
be there. And one minute she is at Belfast airport and
boarding an Easy Jet and the next she is sitting on her
own in London in an abortion clinic waiting room and
you know what? She would rather not be there either.
She would rather be back behind the bar at The Crown,
sloshing beer and pouring pints, with the roar of rau-
cous football cheers and banter. Laughing with the reg-
ulars and smoking out the back. She would rather be

bleeding anywhere, anywhere than here in this white waiting room.

She said, I can do this on my own, and he believed her. He needed to believe it, that she didn't need him, so he wouldn't have to do anything to help. She blames him, she keeps blaming him, but the truth is, she is angrier with herself than him. She should've known better. She's an idiot. A stupid girl. And all of this self-loathing isn't productive, but it floods in epic waves.

While she is in London, she stays at her aunty's in Clapham. She sleeps in the lilac box room, it's all lavender, with a single bed, lace curtains, and a crucifix nailed on the wall above her head. She must be mindful to tiptoe to the bathroom in the night. She must hide any paperwork or clues. She cannot tell her elderly aunty the truth, her mother's sister is too nice, she is of another generation, the old generation. She imagines how the conversation would go if she ever had the guts to tell her:

Aunty, you know, I've a funny story to tell. So, about a month ago, I went to the doctors with a bit of a tummy ache, they ran tests and said, 'You do know you're six weeks pregnant don't you?' No. I laughed and then I cried. No. Of course I didn't know. I've still been getting my period as normal and I had no idea! Isn't that a funny story!

No there is no way to spin it. Her aunty would be utterly appalled, she would think it was her own stupid fault and then that God was punishing her. Her aunty wouldn't let her stay in the house if she knew the true purpose of her trip to London. She tells her aunty she's

24

come for blood tests, she tells her aunty it's nothing to worry about. Her aunty is a bit deaf, she nods and says she is pleased to have a visit from her favourite niece.

She gets ready for the first appointment. She's both nervous and afraid. She takes a minicab and London is all building sites and road works. Her mind isn't on the view though, nor the thick morning traffic, it's on this thing growing inside her.

She will make no attachments. No. She will not guess a gender. No. Nor imagine its soft and perfect tiny fingers reaching up to touch her face. No. She will not feel any tenderness. Stop. She will not dream about a small hot fist curling around her thumb. No. She will not. No, she hasn't. Stop.

At the clinic she takes the abortion pill. It makes her feel a little weak and sleepy at first, as her belly prepares to become a battleground.

Then she can't see for the searing migraine that overtakes her, the bright colourful spots before her eyes. The show is bloody vivid red and dark black, cherry juice, burgundy, red wine and liver. She stares down at it all, she is fascinated that that is what all the fuss is about. She feels no horror but a relief. She says good-bye and is allowed to go home, back to her aunty's. But it's at the follow-up appointment the next week that the doctor says there is something wrong. It isn't normal. Something isn't right.

This is not usual, the doctor says, something is wrong, he says something isn't right.

She sits alone and waits. She looks around the waiting room at the faces of the other women, women who may be in trouble like her. They look like real women, real adult women. Look! There's a real woman, a real lady, and look how her husband strokes her back and pats her hand. And there's another, that girl over there, she is a good and nice girl too. When they call her name, Lucy, her partner rises and holds her hand and goes into the examination room with her. Lucky Lucy.

She sits alone and waits. She hasn't told anyone. She can do this on her own. She will do all this on her own. She can and she will. She repeats these statements as she flicks through a magazine at pictures of kitchen and bathroom makeovers, it makes no sense. She isn't normal. It isn't normal. What is wrong with her? What is wrong with the scan? Why do they need another blood test?

At night at her aunty's, in the lavender room, she has nightmares. She sees a baby boy in blue, gurgling in a cot. Then she dreams she changes his nappy and it's such a stink she cannot breathe, she collapses from the smell, as though it is a fatal poisonous gas. She dreams that the child is a poison, slowly killing her.

Her days become an endless juggling of pain management and cramps, the bleeding and the dread, an awful fear, and waves of shame. She hides some of her used sanitary towels from her aunty, she wraps them up in a plastic bag and puts them in a box under her bed and disposes of them outside when her aunty goes out. She sits with a hot water bottle and aches and stares at daytime television and videos on YouTube. She reads books, but the words blur and swirl before her. She constantly googles her predicament and looks for cases like hers, the after-effects of the abortion pill? She isn't normal. What is normal?

Two weeks pass, and then three, she hardly ever leaves her aunty's house, she binge-watches box sets and cooks nice dinners for her aunty. Sometimes in the evenings they play draughts or cards and have a sherry. Her auntie believes she has the hot water bottle because her appendix is hurting. She takes a minicab to her hospital appointments because it is too painful to walk too far.

At the hospital she is sitting in the waiting room, again. She looks out of the window and can see people enjoying the sunshine, laughing and drinking outside pubs, sitting in groups and smiling in the sun. She watches the summer world outside and remembers it has been so long since she rode a bike. She promises she will ride a bike when she is well, one day, she will ride a bike in the sunshine again, with her feet off the pedals and the breeze in her hair.

And then one afternoon she impulsively orders a beautiful dress online. It is the kind of dress a happily pregnant woman would wear. It is the kind of beautiful dress a good girl would buy when she is blushing and blooming. When people might say that a girl is glowing, blossoming, like an English rose. The maternity dress arrives in the post and she goes upstairs to try it on. She stands and stares at her reflection in the narrow hallway mirror. It is cotton, so soft and long, it flows all the way to the floor, with lots of room for a bump. It's patterned with blue cornflowers, a nice girl might wear a dress like this whilst holding hands with her strong, reassuring, loving husband, as they beam and say in unison, we have some good news, as they collectively produce a photo of a scan at a summer family barbecue.

She starts to wear this dress when her aunty goes out. She wears it in private and in secret, and she daydreams, she imagines what would have happened if things were different, if things were normal. She eyes herself in her dress in the mirror alone and admires her voluptuous shape, her plump breasts, the round belly through the material. But her bump is not normal. The scans and weekly blood tests make no sense. She is still positively pregnant. How can it be? None of it makes any sense.

There is a word the doctors use now: ectopic.

It is lost. She gets lost down hospital corridors. There are forms to fill out. She is asked a volley of questions in the waiting room in front of the other patients. The good girls, the decent and married and normal ladies, all stare and listen and she knows they are listening and that they must think she is a slut and that she is bad and she is alone and she did something wrong and she is not normal. She feels their judgments, she looks down at her ugly, hard, rough feet, jagged and chipped toenails, in cheap plastic flip-flops, dirty feet, dirty girl. This shame is an unbearable heat prickling and creeping up her spine and neck. She sweats, she can feel them all looking and listening behind her.

When was your last bleed?

The nurse asks loud and clear and curtly, holding her cocked biro. She tries to explain that she has had a miscarriage. She has been bleeding for weeks. And all the good girls and nice ladies' ears prick up. They are all quietly judging her, clocking her broad Irish accent, know-

ing that she is so desperate and vulnerable. She wants to cry as she bites her lip but instead she just mumbles,
I'm bleeding now.

Another week has passed and it is another Wednesday. This time she has been asked to fast for twenty-four hours before the examination. She is nauseous and faint, hot and cold at once, she takes off her jacket as she approaches the reception desk. This time, this nurse, cannot find her name on the list, she stares at the computer screen blankly. Types and then stares some more. She asks her to spell it out, twice, and then again. Her name is Aoife but people seem to have difficulty pronouncing and spelling it here in England.

She imagines shouting: A.O.I.F.E.

Seriously now, I promise I am meant to be here, even if I am not on your list, would I make it up that I have an appointment? Do you think I get my kicks by coming here and having a camera inserted into my cunt every Wednesday?

And it has been every Wednesday for six weeks now. Something is wrong, something is very wrong and nobody knows what to do, so they just say come back next week, come back next week, come back next week. Aoife is sick, she is sick of it and she is homesick. She sits in the waiting room and looks at the nice people, good girls and clever ladies with their proud healthy bumps and beautiful children and caring husbands and handsome boyfriends and lovely kitchens and pretty bathrooms and she despairs. Somehow Aoife has got lost, she lost her baby, and is now lost down corridors of bad men and bad choices. Actually there was no choice. There is no father or husband in this picture book. There was a fuck, a fuck happened, some careless fucks with a stupid fuck, but he has gone, stupid fuck.

Aoife said she could handle this alone. And so she does, she goes through all of this on her own and in secret. She doesn't even tell her mother back home. She is sure her aunty suspects something and she keeps fobbing her off, she tells her aunty that it's blood tests, that it's her appendix, maybe a bladder infection. She must get her story straight. Blood tests. Appendix. The bladder infection and kidney stone story sounds iffy and she'll only be lectured. She is twenty-seven years old and she should know better. She works and lives in a pub in Belfast, yeah, but she'll always be baby Aoife to her aunty.

Eight weeks, nine weeks pass, and every Wednesday Aoife sits in that hospital waiting room and waits for more results. And every week nothing makes any sense. They scribble things down, notes about notes, her blood results tell the doctors she is pregnant but they cannot find a fetus. How can that be?

The needles hardly hurt anymore, she won't flinch now, her arm is all purple with bruises to prove she is a weekly blood-giving veteran. Each week another blood test and each week she tests positive, pregnant, but with no fetus. And each week more laying back and staring at the white tiled hospital ceiling, legs spread as a cool plastic camera is inserted, and each week yet another doctor saying,

Just taking a quick look inside, that's a good girl, now this might be cold, this might pinch, breathe out and relax as much as you can…

She laughs about it, now, as she makes the same joke, she tells each new doctor that she must be Mary, mother of Jesus and the holy ghost.

You do know that I am Mary? She laughs. Now you see it and now you don't. Yes. She knows this is blasphemy, but fuck the Pope, she could have stayed in Belfast for treatment if Ireland wasn't stuck in the dark ages. If it wasn't so complicated. If any of this were normal.

Aoife starts to feel a little better. She has made friends and gets familiar with some members of staff. In hospitals you notice the kindest nurses right away, and God, thank God for them, because this is the stuff they don't tell you about, this is the bit a girl will have to do mostly on her own, this is the loneliest journey any woman ever has to make. This is the train journey that stops at the desolate stations we call:

Split Condom. Missed Pill. Mistake. Abortion. Miscarriage. Ectopic.

At Aoife's last appointment in London the doctor shows her a scan. This time, this doctor, he is particularly helpful and kind. His voice is soft and calm. He turns the television screen towards her and shows her a black-and-white pulsing image. And now for the first time she sees inside herself and she sees something, a pale and ghostly shape, as the doctor explains,

See this shadow, here? Here on the outside, that shape, I believe that's where your truth was, and you see, that's all that matters, but here this dark patch, this is where you put blame, and this is where your choice was, but other people's guilt and shame began to grow, it's all gone now, faded, but that is what was causing you all that pain, your heart was trying to live on the outside. Your reason and your truth tried to grow outside here, look, see, like a wild flower, like a cornflower growing between the cracks in a concrete path… You'll be right as rain now.

Aoife returns to Belfast and returns to herself, the pain fades, the memories dim, some of the guilt dilutes. But guilt, my love, she says, that's a choice, you can torture yourself with that for years to come if you choose to stare into the playgrounds of what could have been. And late at night, drinking whiskey in the back kitchen of the pub, you'll hear the girls of The Crown, all laughing and conspiring and whispering to each other as Aoife spills her heart out, pours her story straight, sharing the truth between sips of mother's milk, she begins,

Did I ever tell you what really happened that summer I went to London?

Aoife hugs the new barmaid, she's been crying, she's a girl in trouble with nobody to talk to. Aoife makes sure all the girls of the neighbourhood can come to her from now on, she says, all over the world, this is the stuff they don't tell you about, this is the bit a girl will mostly have to do on her own, this is the loneliest choice any woman ever has to make, but it is her choice. Women are elastic, how miraculous we are, how the female body swells and grows and then springs back to you, as you come home to yourself.

Aoife wipes the bar top as she sings: What don't kill me only makes me stronger. Goodbye to the used and the abused, the battered and bruised, scars like train tracks, clothes like potato sacks. Goodbye to tarnished tin soldiers, the cowboys that cried, the washed-up pirates. And goodbye to the broken-nosed boxer who could have been a contender. She sings, bring me the half full and never the half empty.

It is a Wednesday and Aoife rides a red bicycle. She glides downhill, with her feet off the pedals and the wind in her hair. She sails in a long soft dress, billowing, patterned with blue cornflowers. Summer is done and September arrives with gentle time, with auburn and red leaves, with a soft golden light.

kali

kajal odedra

Krishna sat next to her brother, holding his hand, handling conversation topics like shiny objects on a shopping channel. Anything to engage him. Raju was unresponsive, looking despondent, as though the entire day's ceremony had nothing to do with him. He sat in the corner of the room staring at the TV, rolling Indian news, sound washing over him, as if watching the sea, mesmerised by the moving images. At twenty-five he was a grown man. When he stood he towered over his mother and sister. In the last year he had gained weight that gathered at his belly, making it protrude; making his mud green C&A jumper stretch. He looked like a child who had outgrown his clothes.

The family fussed around him as the others arrived: his aunt, uncle, and grandmother. Raju remained still in the corner as the room played on fast-forward: tidying, searching, preparing. He looked like he was on pause.

On the surface this looked like any other family gathering hosted at the Sainis' home. Raju's mother had grown three pairs of hands as she boiled rice, flipped chapati, and crushed garlic to make enough food to feed a village. But unlike previous gatherings, there were no cars spilling out of the driveway and lining this tiny street in the middle of Birmingham. No children running from room to room, under tables, through legs. There were few guests, only close family; no one could know this was happening. Unlike at other gatherings, the mood was sombre. The weight of the occasion hung over them all like lead.

Tones were hushed as the family gathered in the living room, cross-legged on the floor. At that moment the living room door opened and in came a small older woman. The room tensed. The reason for the gathering could no longer be avoided. She moved slowly, the old lady. Her lilac cotton sari cloaked her lowered head, her greying hair pulled back in a bun with thick white strands straggling free. Her skin was dark, darker than most who sat in the room. And it was wrinkled, making the woman look twisted, like she'd been squeezed, stretched. Raju's mother fussed to make a clearing, a stiff smile and wide eyes giving up her nerves. She ushered Krishna into the kitchen to bring in a chair and place it in the middle of the room. The woman smiled politely, declining the chair. She sat on the floor, her legs crossed, baring her rough, drying feet with crooked toenails that looked centuries old.

When Krishna had come home from university that week, she had found Raju in the same spot, in the corner of the living room staring at the TV. His eyes looked drunk—red and blurry. There used to be white around his iris, now there was off-white, almost yellow. Two years older than her, Raju had always felt like her younger brother. When they were eight and ten their parents questioned the children about a suspicious phone bill: unknown numbers listed, each call lasting a few seconds. Krishna knew this had nothing to do with her and Raju because they shared everything. They spent every moment together, sharing a room, sharing secrets. They would stay up late, with their beds pushed together, inventing games. Raju loved the one where they drew pictures on each other's backs; you had to guess what the picture was, following the slow, steady tracing of a finger. It tickled but was never unbearable. It was soft and comforting. She had been confused when she overheard her mother crying to their father that she had caught Raju in the act, making phone calls to women he found in the phone book. Listening to them speak and then hanging up. She heard her mother crying about sharam. The Shame. Krishna didn't understand. If it was a game why didn't they play it together? The phone calls stopped. It was never mentioned.

When their father died suddenly, four years later, everyone told Raju he had to be the Man Of The House. He was just a teenager. The weight of his future felt crippling. He couldn't do it. Krishna watched him with-

draw. He became quiet. That was when they grew apart.
"Raju, how are you doing? Have you been to work this
week?" Krishna asked her brother softly. As though in
slow motion, he turned from the screen to his sister.
Looking vacant, he smiled.

"Krish. Krish, you came. Can you help me? I can't find
my watch. Mum said she looked, but I don't think she
really looked. Will you help?" His arms stretched out.
Krishna crouched down to the seat to hug her brother.
Her heart sank. She could smell body odour mixed with
the smell of food and the mustiness of clothes worn for
days. She felt the fat his body had gained since she last
saw him. In the year that she had been studying medicine at Imperial College, Raju had been married and di-
vorced. Their mother had his marriage quickly arranged,
worried about what would become of her declining son.
It was difficult to find a family who would take on a boy
as shy and awkward as Raju, so after searching in the
UK, she gave up and arranged his marriage to a village
girl from Gujarat. This was a sure bet, everyone knew
that village girls were desperate for a British passport.
During this time, Krishna got a phone call from Raju
out of the blue.

"How's uni, Krish?" The music in his voice, his melody and rhythm, had flattened. He never called. She knew
this wasn't just a check-in.

"How are you, Raju, and mum, and work? Everything
okay over there?" He had got a job working in their uncle's mini-mart, managing the shop floor. The job was
given out of loyalty and put their mum's mind at ease,
knowing her son was working.

"Mum said I should speak to you. I don't want to get married, Krish, she said you'll help me understand." He blurted out the words and then fell silent. Raju wasn't used to asking for things, and this was a plea for help. Krishna could hear how naked and vulnerable he felt as soon as the words left his mouth. Hot tears blurred her vision. She blinked to force them away.

"I don't know, Raju, maybe this is a good plan for you. What else will you do?"

"Work with uncle? Mum says I should marry because people will talk if I don't. But I don't want that, Krish."

Her heart ached. She wanted to protect him. "What is the girl like? Does she seem nice?" This was a futile question: Raju had spent ten minutes on the phone with his prospective bride while his mother sat at his side. They talked about their parents and siblings. They discussed what they did on the weekends, which wasn't a lot; the conversation felt strained and they were struggling for topics. Krishna agreed to speak to their mother, to persuade her to relax, let Raju be for a few more years. He wasn't living up to his mother's expectations, but Krishna could see he was content, working with his uncle, who was like a father to Raju, and coming home to play football on his computer. Her brother was a late developer; maybe he would mature later than her. But Krishna's words fell on deaf ears, and a month later Raju was flown to India to marry Shilpa, who spoke broken English and had never lived away from home.

Raju's new bride was homesick almost as soon as she arrived in the UK. She pined for the security of familiar things, the soft feel of an old ten-rupee note, the heat of the dusty floor at midday on her bare feet. She missed squatting to go to the toilet. Chopping vegetables in the morning sun. But she kept quiet and subservient, cooking and cleaning the house to pass the time, all the while growing bitter toward her groom. Six months passed and something snapped. Shilpa left Raju. *How could this happen, after just a few months? Why hadn't he asked his mother to help?* He couldn't answer his mother's desperate questions. Shilpa moved in with family in Leicester, and soon it was rumoured that they had never consummated their marriage. Though Raju's mother tried hard to make Shilpa part of the family, she couldn't resolve what was happening behind their bedroom door. Losing control and fiercely protective, Raju's mother confronted Shilpa. She heard what had gone on in that year, how they slept on opposite sides of the bed.

"He doesn't touch me, sasu, how do you expect a woman to live like this? How do you expect me to give you grandchildren?"

"Shilpa betty, we work on these things. Men are different to us, we have to be patient."

They were desperate, the both of them, convinced that Raju needed help. But their idea of help was at odds, and they came to no resolution.

Gossip within the community was like tar: it reeked and was impossible to remove. Raju was stained. It was never mentioned in their house again. By the time Krishna returned home, her brother had been broken by the power of the women around him. His innocence was battered, and he sat vacant, on rewind; the same seat, every day, staring at the TV screen.

*

"He's not the same." Krishna's mother looked like she hadn't slept, her brown eyes sunken like two wells.

"He's been through so much—dad's death, a divorce."

"Don't talk about divorce! He hasn't said one word about that! He stopped washing, he complains about a headache every day. And now for the last few weeks, he only asks for you." Krishna's mother had a hand on her forehead or her chest whenever she spoke these days, as though she was clutching her heart and head to stop them from spilling open.

"Something has happened to him. I told your uncle to take him to the temple. God is our only help now."

"What did the doctor say?"

"Your uncle spoke to the priest, he said Raju might be possessed. He's not himself. It's in his soul, Krishna, it's dark. Something bad has got hold of him. I asked your auntie, what did I do? What did I do wrong?"

"You haven't taken him to Dr Patel have you?"

"Your auntie thinks maybe I spoke ill against Bhagavan. It's my fault. I've cursed Raju." Her mother's eyes filled with tears. "But the priest said this happens. It happened to your second cousin's wife in India, Vali. Did you hear about that? They ignored it, they did nothing, she was just like Raju, losing her mind. Oh Vali, poor Vali! Krishna, they found her in her house, she hung herself. She had two little babies." Krishna wondered if her mother was enjoying the drama.

"Mum, please promise not to speak like this in front of him. You think he's ill because you spoke against

God? This kind of talk is what's making him ill. We need to get him on antidepressants, some exercise—"

"Shame on you, Krishna! You want to give your brother drugs, antidepressants! No son of mine is going to the doctor to tell him he is crazy. He isn't himself, you don't understand these things. I told you the priest said it's happened before to people in the community. Something bad has got in his soul. *Pey*, it's a bad spirit. The priest will help us, thank God, thank Rama, thank Sita. He knows a lady who can look at him."

*

Krishna had tried to stop her mother from arranging the ceremony. But, like a woman possessed, or a mother in the grips of desperation, she had stopped listening to the protests. In the days leading up to it they had talked every night, her mother haunted with the thought that she had cursed her family. Since returning from university, Krishna had noticed the growing presence of God in their house. It grew like the moon, until it was only possible to see in its own light. Her mother, who had always been religious but never a zealot, had taken to spending more time at the shrine dedicated to Ganesh, the Remover of Obstacles. She sat there for hours, lighting balls of cotton wool soaked in oil, waving incense, rearranging the monuments. She wasn't sleeping, but spent hours on the phone to her sister, talking about God. Was she cursed? She had lost her husband and now her son. The Shame. When Krishna heard her mother mutter over and over about sharam and izzat, obsessing about covering up the family's shame, keeping their honour, she began to see the illusion of their community unravel. It was a lie to create control, and it was poisonous. It was poisoning her family. Running through every possibility, her mother managed to pinpoint the exact moment when she had made remarks about one of the gods; she had spoken ill of Kali, the Goddess of Destruction, and now she was being punished. She started to pray to a picture of Kali every morning, a black figure with a necklace of heads, skirt of arms, and lolling tongue. Kali's image was violent. She was dishevelled and chaotic, and the value placed on her in their household made even a picture in a frame seem dangerous. Krishna felt on edge around it but never mentioned this to her mother, who begged for Kali's forgiveness. She often sat in silence in the living room, clutching prayer beads between her fingers, rubbing them while muttering words of devotion to the gods under her breath. It was her mother who had wanted Krishna to be a doctor, pressured her to study medicine, "get a good job, good salary." Doctors were respected. But she refused to let her son see one. It was The Shame.

In the days leading up to the ceremony Krishna had spent time with her brother. He was a different person to the boy she had grown up with. He spent hours lying in his dank, musty bed. He sobbed about the headaches, so she took to placing cold, wet flannels on his forehead. It was no surprise, Krishna thought, that he was taking comfort in the Gita too. For most of the day she would find him with the book on his lap, his index finger following each line, devouring every word. She asked him if he wanted to see the doctor.

"Mum says I'm not crazy. God will make this go away."

She thought about madness. About what she had expected it to look like. That nobody really knows it until it's there in front of you. The hysteria her mother was creating, that was madness, she thought.

*

The woman in the lilac sari opened a carrier bag and placed copies of the Gita to her right. She took out a container of olive oil, a purple packet of incense, and a spray bottle of water and placed them to her left. She pointed at Raju and beckoned him over. Raju had snapped out of his trance for the first time since Krishna had been home. He looked around the room, taking in what was happening, his eyes welling up. Krishna held tightly onto her brother's hand. Their aunt marched over and pulled his other hand, pushing him to the centre of the room. The lady took a copy of the Gita and began to read from it, her voice tense and twisted like her skin, chanting passages for several minutes. She had full command of the room. Raju, opposite, looking to the ground as reams of Sanskrit spilled from her mouth. The words were like weights, pulling him down into the ground; with every syllable Krishna felt it would be harder to lift him up. A silky, dark, wrinkled hand placed on Raju's forehead pushed him down to her feet while she was chanting. When she had his head firmly to the carpet she fell silent, closing her eyes, her hand still pressed to his head.

She shrieked. A high-pitched and wobbly cry, unsettling everyone in the room. Her small black eyes opened, two shiny beads staring down at Raju. She asked the spirit slowly for its name. She was speaking to Raju as though he was the devil. His eyes were wide and he held his mouth in a grimace. He was barely breathing. Once, when they were little, Raju had pushed Krishna with more force than he realised, sending her toppling into the fireplace with the fire burning. Raju's face had crumpled into devastation. Krishna was mildly burnt but Raju was scarred, mortified at what he had done. He was inconsolable. He cried until he fell asleep that night. His pillow soaked and his heart exhausted. He looked like that boy now.

The lady began rocking side to side, chanting faster and louder. Side to side to side to side. Chanting faster and louder and louder. The swaying and volume grew and grew, and then stopped. That's when the sobbing began. Krishna's mother now poured into the chaos, sobbing quietly. Her sobs turned to prayers. Her aunt rushed across the room to comfort her sister, stroking her head to her breast and swaying side to side like the old lady. The whole room felt like it was swaying side to side. Raju now lay horizontally on the floor. The old lady was squatting over him and waving lit sticks of incense over his body, drawing lines of smoke over his face. Her tight white bun was breaking free and her sari had come loose, hanging from her shoulder, waving around like a third arm. An unruly Ganesh. The sound of the number eight bus rolling down the road leaked into their private ceremony, the bus braking at the stop opposite their house, and then the engine started again and it rode away. There was a world out there that didn't know what was happening on this street on the outskirts of the city. In this semidetached house with a Ford Mondeo parked outside. Krishna wanted to gasp for air. The room was suffocating, the smell of patchouli from the incense thick and sweet, like a patchouli-soaked cloth being stuffed down her throat.

"Aatma! Chale jao!" The lady now had her hands pressed on Raju's chest. She was screaming at the spirit, telling it to leave.

"Chale jao!"

The room seemed smaller, like the walls had moved in. Krishna wanted to pick Raju up and lead him out of there. She looked at her mother, aunt, uncle, and grandmother, they were all gripped. There was hope in their eyes. Her uncle was nodding, urging the lady to win in this battle against evil. Her grandmother looked like she was watching a soap opera. Her face was animated, though this wasn't really happening to real people, right in front of her. Looking down at her brother, Krishna saw that he had zoned out again. His eyes glazed over, staring at the ceiling.

*

After the ceremony, the old lady was taken into the kitchen for tea and biscuits. Sitting at the table sipping

45

at their saucers, the older women made small talk, as though wrapping up a business deal.

"How is the rest of family, all good?"

"Yes, yes. Daughter is studying medicine at a very good university. Imperial College. She will be a doctor soon!"

"A doctor, very good. Very important. You will find her a good husband."

Krishna helped Raju to his feet. His face wet with tears, he looked at his sister like he was five years old and had fallen off his bike. He slowly sat down on the sofa in the corner of the room. He stared at the TV and began swaying, side to side. Krishna placed her palm to her forehead; her head had started to ache. She needed a cold flannel. Was the madness catching? Raju sat, his mouth hanging slightly open, but he wasn't speaking. She crouched down next to him.

"Raju, how are you feeling?" He didn't look at her this time. He began tapping himself on his chest.

"Is it gone now?"

"I don't know, Raju. Does it feel like it's gone?"

*

A week had passed and, though she felt strange about returning to university, Krishna felt a little relieved to be leaving. She went into Raju's room to say good-bye, but he wasn't in there. She hadn't looked in his room for a few days. It was different. The sheets were fresh, the curtains open. His clothes, which had usually been piled in a heap like a creature at the end of his bed, were folded on his chest of drawers, ready to be put away. She went downstairs to look for him and found both Raju and her mother in the kitchen doing chores together. In the last few weeks, the house had felt like it was feeding off chaos, the walls, the furniture absorbing and breeding insanity. Now Raju sat at the kitchen table pouring spices into containers. Their mother was at the other end of the table organising the nice crockery into sets. They both seemed less frantic. Raju was still subdued but laughing at his mother's jokes. His state was less trancelike. He was aware of his surroundings, comfortable moving around. He seemed less distressed, almost at peace. Krishna had expected a fight until her last day to persuade her mother to take Raju to the doctor. But as the days passed, this seemed unnecessary. He had even started to shower and was eating with the family at mealtimes. He was still clutching the Gita; it never left his side. He would spend time each morning and evening reading it quietly in his room. And their mother continued to devote hours each day to her religious shrine, constantly rubbing the wooden balls of her beads between her thumb and index finger.

Krishna was waiting for Raju to slip, to break down and need her help. But he never did. She thought the spiritual ceremony would traumatise him, but in the days after he seemed calmer. He was becoming more devout, but she could hardly fault his newfound focus and patience. She should have felt relieved, happy for him. But she felt guilty, that she wanted to be right. She was ashamed that a medicine woman had been allowed into their home and had helped her brother. That this had happened in her own home in Britain, not a regressive village in India. That he was fast becoming dedicated to religion. She should have felt relieved to go back to university knowing her brother was at peace and her mother at ease. But Krishna felt like she had lost. Before she left she asked her mother whether the medicine woman would be back.

"Krishna, let's pray that the spirit never comes back. I can't afford to bring her in again, and I don't think we need to. He is getting what he needs from God."

"We paid her?"

"Of course we paid her, Krishna. She has a special gift from God, she needs to be supported. We must give these people our complete respect. And that doesn't matter now. Look at him, I think he might go back to work soon. Thank Rama, we must thank Rama every day. And you, you thought your brother was crazy."

shitluck

martin de mello

It looks like a dried slug, the same one I poured salt on the other day. Probably it died on the doorstep and someone trod on it and brought it in on her shoe. I'll have words. Next to it on the lino there's a bitten-off fingernail. Not mine, I would recognise. She must've been biting her nails while she stood at the door.

At my feet a single, unhappy leaf. Like, I think it's turned yellow, yellowish, I can't quite tell. My little yellow friend.

That's why I like sitting here. The uncertainty, murkiness. Streetlight tapping on the window above the door. When you sit here everything is kind of muddy shadow.

And draft. You feel it most at the bottom of the stairs. Heavy, like, you know, when you were a kid and the shadow of the school bully appeared on the tarmac next to yours. And you got that sick feeling in your stomach. Different school, same bullying. That's not how my old man saw it. He reckoned a white man and a black man don't cast the same shadow. I guess he knew what he was saying. Not that he gave a shit. Spent the whole of his life going nowhere. And me, I don't appear to be going anywhere. And Tara. What about her?

She's got a mouth like a bitch.

The draft, yeah, it's type of flipping one side of the leaf every now and again, like the turning page of a newspaper. Forward and back. The other half must be stuck to the floor. If you bother to notice things like leaves in the first place. Probably, if I got down on my hands and knees and listened to it, it would be making a noise like a cockroach. Like, you know, dirty, ready to hide, skittering.

Probably that's the noise it's making right now but I can't fucking hear it cos the dog over the road is barking. Won't shut the fuck up. Like, since seven thirty, eight o'clock. Mary, Holy Mother of God. It's in competition with the Duracell bunny. Fuck knows what a dog has to bark about but I can tell you for free it lives in a yard full of gnomes, in the middle of which is a statue of Jesus. Probably that's it, it's not barking at all. Probably it's speaking in tongues. Asking God what it should do about the cats. God doesn't answer, so it asks God's representative. The representative says kill them all, God will know his own. And you and me both know where that goes.

None of which answers the question: what the fuck does a dog have to bark about? Nor the question: what do we?

Even if we did there's no point. It doesn't change anything. Three doors down have a staf what nobody's stolen yet. I ain't never heard it make any sound. It just shits all over the back yard and brings it into the house. They leave the back door open, let it run in and out and don't give a fuck. Like, how they live with the smell? You can't sit in your backyard of an evening because of it. I complained. The other neighbours complained. As per, the council won't do anything. That's our problem. Just like with the potholes. At least the gnome owners clean their yard. Religiously. I mean, that's how I think of it. Crossing themselves and saying prayers. There's that thing about cleanliness.

Me, my opinion is that regardless of shit, dogs are dirty. I can't understand how anyone has them in the house. Tara has a different opinion. She says you can't blame an animal for being itself.

What about me?

Apparently, I'm not an animal.

Now ask me what she wants.

Or don't ask, it's not like I care. I don't make a point of remembering things. I'm simple like that. I know that dog barks and bites. Tara remembers the exact date it had puppies. Like, who remembers that shit? Bark and bite. Half nature, the other half. They got a Beware of the Dog sign on the gate, that's all you need to know. Patrolling, forward and back. And my guy mistreats her, keeps her mean. You can see it in her eyes. Look over the fence and the bitch will be there starin at you, trowel twiddling in hand.

You gotta stare back, that's your only choice. Even on the days when my vision is blurred.

Then she'll have that squint in her eyes. You don't even know her but she knows everything she needs to know about you. That's what that squint is. Contempt. English contempt. She won't say it to your face though. To your face it's that fuck-off politeness. Like we give a shit, I mean we all fucking hate her. You don't get to own the franchise on hatred just cos you were born white. I don't know you, I didn't decide to sneer every time you walked past. You can have it back in return. For fuck's sake, even the Buddhists hate her. They hide it behind the bouncy castle they keep in their front garden. Just cos all the local kids hang about with their kid, Lien. Bounce about, I should say. That don't disguise the fact that the bouncy castle is a wall.

Keep out. So we do.

Lien doesn't do walls, though. She talks to squinty face. Talks to everyone. You're minding your own business and suddenly she'll be there next to you chattering away about what she did at school or what she's having for tea or do you eat enough because you're so thin. Says her, who looks like a piece of string. I mean, she looks like when she was born they tried pullin her arms and legs off. They kind of dangle a bit and you don't really notice until she runs, like her legs swing loose at the hips and her arms kind of wriggle about somewhere behind her. And she understands everything you say even though she's partially deaf.

Yeah, she'll talk about anything that one. But her favouritest thing in the whole wide world is cats. Fucking

52

A. If she catches one she'll bring it to you. Yeah, that's a cat. And the cat knows it's a cat. And all the neighbourhood cats know her. That's why they run. And she'll run after them.

That's how Lien nearly got killed.

About this time last year the ginger tom saw her coming, skipped across the road and she skipped after it. No cares, like Fish from the crew at the end of the road, redlining his wheels from a standing start. The only reason he didn't kill her was cos he took evasive action. Two cars totalled and a fractured skull. Got three months for that. Didn't knock any sense though. Wasn't no twocker when he went in but sure enough knew how to twock when he came out. Didn't learn any better how to drive. That's prison for ya.

Wonderful world, beautiful people.

That said he's still young. Still time to learn. We've all been there. That's why our endz is our endz. Hood. Whatever the fuck you want to call it. You probably know it anyway, from the TV or something. One of them police reality shows. It's true, we're all the same. I am them and they are me, though some of them might be twenty years younger. Makes it confusing, being in a hood full of doppelgangers. At least no one needs a mirror.

And bonus, you don't have to ask yourself every day what is real?

Real is whatever they are. Real is the sound of that fucking dog. Not giving up. Barking and its bark type of making dots in the hallway. Each bark becomes a dot on the wall and each morning the girl child finds them, joins them up and turns them into pictures. One of the drawings is a dinosaur. It's meant to be a stegosaurus but it looks like a hedgehog on stilts. There's this little man runnin like shit so he doesn't get eaten, sticky legs at right angles, and the moon near the top of the door cos it should be little and white and not get in the way.

Cos that's what the moon does, get in the way.

Maybe that's harsh but once you notice. It just hangs there like someone shot a hole in the night and it hasn't died yet. It keeps me awake, especially when the pain won't go away.

They told me hydromorphone would work. Truth is there aren't many nights when it does. Or many nights when that dickferbrain cracker isn't shoutin at someone to fuck off.

I mean seriously. Him and the dog. Except he's forty, wears shitluck and he earned it. Big man, still lives with his mama. So far this year has got a fifteen year old pregnant. If I were her old man I'd have knocked his front teeth out. Exceptin they drink together and piss together. And go to the massage parlour. Which is where he met her.

You never really know anyone, that's what I take away from that. Exceptin I know him. His list includes time for assault, theft, more time for assault, time for handling stolen goods, for possession, time for fraud and time for no other reason than sheer utter stupidity.

I guess he has a point when he asks why the police keep picking on him?

Cos he's a handsome motherfucker.

Looks good in the baseball cap his mama brought him back from America, and that fat-arse gold chain. Looks fucking good. All five foot half an inch of him.

The assaults were domestic by the way. That's all the information you need to know.

It won't help that he started off in a flat on his own as a single dad. Lasted three years like that. Problem for him was that he kept sticking it in. Nine kids, six baby-mothers, I think. His eldest boy committed suicide and the last three are in care. Shaz, the first girl, seemed like he wanted her. Anyways, she disappeared in Glasgow. I did hear she made it to university. Not sure I believe that, not that believing is really the point. Maybe some-one's still waiting for her.

I doubt very much he thinks about any of this. That noise now is him challenging someone to a fight. He does it by tellin them, "Fuck off, you wanna ruck?" And then when they square up he grabs his arse and takes it indoors. There must be a disease in his heart. He might come back with a knife, he's been known to do that. He might wake up in the morning and find three guys with baseball bats parked up, waiting for him. Or his mama might come out and settle the argument. She don't take no crap from no one, which type of makes it more of a shame. I mean, how the fuck did she end up with him?

But then we ask ourselves these questions every day. Probably the alcohol had something to do with it. Her and me both. We have the livers to prove it.

That's how it is, that's how its always gonna be, what-ever the fuck any government says. Different day, same shit. I can't blame him. Exceptin his mama no one paid attention to him, he ain't gonna pay attention to them. You could bring the Queen down here, every fucker would love her but no one would believe a word that she said.

That's a test you can apply to yourself. Belief.

Me? Will this pain just please go away. Even I shift my arse up a step I can't get my leg properly straight. It's like my knee's rusted shut.

—Yo, nice blades man, where ya get em from?

I didn't hear her pull up. Usually she makes a grand entrance. For someone that works at Greggs she's doin well. Spare cash to pimp. Audi, I think. The blades she gets from this guy Hassan, who gets them from Nev, who gets them from some smackhead in Liverpool. They're probably recycled between cities. Eighteen inches. The ride's type of nervous with the low profiles but she can spin on a bottle top. And outrace every manboy around here.

—Fuck me man, where's ya get dat hoo ride? Muh wheels'll rip da arse offa dat ting.

Mr five foot half an inch is back in town. Whoever he was arguing with must have better things to do. And for a man what has his arse hangin out of a Corsa.

—Yo, white boy, she nineteen, blood. Too old for ya boo.

And too much sense. His last two pickney were from the same babymother. I don't know what the term is but she was disabled, simple. For whatever reason he ended up with them. Or rather his mama did. She went off for the weekend with her squeeze and he left them with a tin of baked beans and lit out. When his mama got back and he wasn't there, straight she phoned social services. When it came to it he wouldn't drag his white arse into court.

That's what I've seen, and for everything that's happened to him he's still a knob. The local celebrity. Whatever he does there's an audience. Dancing in front of a sofa, shitfaced. Mind, the sofa was in the middle of the park and on fire at the time. We were all sat around, Blaze popping a tune, sharing joints, us humming along if we knew the words. And there he was dancing mental to whatever song was going on inside his head. He stripped naked and half the neighbourhood was there watching him. Fucking lunatic. It burned good, the sofa, flames rising out of the ground. We were twenty feet away and the heat was enough. Then the fire brigade arrived, put it out, and we all went back to our homes. Left him whimpering in the darkness.

Probably one of us should've helped him. Not me, that ain't no job for a cripple. It worked out anyway. There was a thunderstorm that night. When I hung out the window he was back on his porch with his fingers in his ears arguing with his mother. For some weird reason every time there was lightning he kinda flopped out into the road, then his mama went out to fetch him and they'd start the whole thing again. Shit like that really asks questions of you. It looked like he was having some kind of religious experience, him and the universe.

And me and the stairs.

A stair warrior, that's me, with a busted leg. Waiting. The stairs are a resting place. A haven. Without a carpet they actually feel like proper stairs, and smell like them. Sometimes they smell like talc, other times musty damp. I think it depends on the weather. Today's smell is bleach. And headaches.

Headaches have a smell too. Mine, when I have a bad one, smell like chlorine. They type of ping inside my sinuses, kind of a grub making its home up there, chewing on my skull. I get a similar effect from next door. Not the fuckwit Indian movies they watch every night but his singing. It'll start, he always starts halfway through the film. His voice is squeaky when you talk to him on the street but when he sings it's like lobbing a brick through a window. He isn't a big man, not that that matters. He likes singing, it's his own home. Whatever noises come through the walls are his business. Don't know her name. They moved in sixteen, seventeen months ago. When I see her we say hi, maybe a couple of words. She looks like an electricity pylon. That's what I thought the first time I saw her. The other thing I noticed was her smile. Whatever god, Krishna or Vishnu, that's their god of smiles.

The Angolan woman, girl actually, she has that smile too. They were separated at birth. I don't think I could live either of their lives. The Angolan girl has a one year old and her house is infested with cockroaches. You go in and they've been crushed into the carpet, even in her bedroom. I think it's a private landlord but she was put there by the Home Office. Me, I'd complain, no one should have to live with that. That's what I told her. She reckons she makes a complaint, bam, she'll be out of Manchester. Her friend complained and they put her in

Blackburn. Wasn't there a week before 'fuck off asylum seeker' had been painted on the front door.

I'd take my chances, rather that than cockroaches. Dirty bastards doin the Harlem Jive. Don't know how she does it. Her family are dead. I can't even contemplate her loneliness.

She smiles anyway. That smile when you know behind it they're really depressed. Tara and her don't get on.

Whatever. If there's a word for her it's beautiful. I told her that, it didn't make any difference. I bought a couple of bottles of wine. You have to try and help somehow.

I can't say the same thing about next door. I mean, I told her what I thought of her smile. Dignified. Me and Mr Squeak had a disagreement about that. I'm not saying he's mean but he's mean. Doesn't like her talking to anyone. Cos I'm gonna hobble round in front of the whole fucking neighbourhood, bringing a stepladder with me so I can climb up it and kiss her on the knees. That's if there's a ten-minute gap when one of his fifty cousins isn't round being fed. I don't know what else she does but definitely she spends a lot of time cooking.

The other thing I know is she comes from a village. My village had a stream. We'd go fishing in it as kids. When I could, before I busted my leg, I'd bike up to the Mersey just so I could sit on the bank. Up at dawn and head even when it was pissing it down. Okay, there were gnats, and gnats are vicious bastards, but the Mersey's the closest round here I can get to that stream. Plenty of time to think, me on my own, sometimes a few guys painting the fences on a Community Service Order. That gig was alright when I got it, better than clearing scrub. Cutting down blackthorn, I wouldn't recommend. Probably I'd start thinking about something I didn't want to think about, then I'd head back and the kid opposite would be playin Prodigy full volume out of his bedroom window. Leanin out, smokin. Looking like a slapped arse.

That's what happens when there's nuthin to do. Me, I don't care for the Prodigy. That shit rubs me the same way the shit next door does. Asha Bhosle off da hook, my guy making noise like a siren. He sounds like that when he gets angry as well. Hard little fists, according to her sunglasses. She had them on yesterday when she told me there's more chickens in the world than people.

–Get the fuck outta muh face man, ya breath stink.

–You callin me?

–You're a cunt, get outta my face, you're a fuckin cunt. He's a cunt, I don't care.

Through the door the scuffle sounds like a small dog trapped in a bath, except that a dog doesn't make a noise like a sack of rice being poured onto a tray, which is my guy bein lick down pon da floor. It's the sound of shit-luck and gold chain faceplanting on concrete.

He bleeds easy, it's the soft doughy face. He'll get up, wrap his fat wedgy fingers round his mouth an go whinin to his mama. And she'll listen, even though he starts every mornin tellin her to go fuck herself.

Fool.

And the dog barkin. Probably it wants to join in.

And me? Truth is.

Truth is everyone fucks up. Cos that's revelation. I'm sat in a hallway facing a door that's not gonna open.

Next to two empty rooms. Not in and not out. Time was.

Time was it wasn't me that was waiting. Knowing everyone on the street, their lives. Hearing the weed on their voices. You can even hear it on their skin. It sounds like crisp packets, like hot knife. Their voices type of fill up the hallway and stick to the wall, changing colour. Splashes of dried green, rattan, bamboo, cow dung, tilapia, catfish, those kinds of colours and shapes. Some of their voices are water, spiders, *bapa*, broken bottles, aftershave, coffee, *bapa*, whatever you can smell or think of, gobs of snot, *bapa*.

The girl child at the top of the stairs, blue eyes and mine brown, blond hair and mine brown, white skin and mine brown. I promised her I'd buy all the love in the world, take her to Auschwitz, to Changhi Point, watch the planes coming in to land so low you can lick them. And her blue eyes the only blue eyes in the world I can read, the only blue eyes in the world I understand, except for my mother's. Only hers are shining blue discs of resentment and the girl child's are tiny blue seas. She's had a bad dream.

—Ah, baby girl.
—Where's Tara?
—I'm waiting for her.
—Why?
—I don't know, to make sure she comes back.
—But why?
—If I don't wait for her she'll disappear. It happens to everyone.

She thinks about that, taps the palm of her hand against her thigh.

—Are you waiting for me?

—I don't have to, baby girl.

—Tell me a story, bapa.

—Come sit here then.

She makes her way down the stairs, hand against the wall.

—Careful, there's a nail sticking out.

She touches my leg.

—You're alright, it's not so bad. Your stegosaurus is still there, you haven't scribbled over it yet.

—I miss her.

—You and me both, darlin. You and me both. Tell me, where do you want your story to begin?

two days and two nights in kisumu

raymond antrobus

"The world in English has sharp edges."
—Binyavanga Wainaina

day 1

The classroom is an open-air hut,
84 children on chairs and low brick walls.
I walk in reeking of the road.
There's a gap in the roof where sunlight
beams onto my forehead.
Hello, I say. *Jambo Bwana*, the class says.
Dan explains, the kids speak Luo and Kiswahili
so he will need to translate.
Even the poets I met in Cape Town
would call this village *the real Africa*
not because the children don't have shoes (they do)
but because there are no hotels
or British schools or Chinese casinos.

Shannon, a girl in a faded Man United shirt
asks how I became a poet.
I start talking in a language distant
until Dan carries my story in his tongue.

night 1

> "Barack Obama is 'part-Kenyan' and has an 'ancestral'
> hatred of Britain."
>
> *—Boris Johnson*

I lie in the candlelit hut
thinking how English
would never be the right tongue
to ask this class what matters.
I wonder what if no European
discovered anything in Kenya?
What if there was no brutal history
to speaking and writing English?
Would they still have
colonised the classroom?

Ben

        John David

                Christine   Hayley

   Toby

day 2

"Wat a devilment a Englan!
Dem face war and brave de worse
But me wonderin how dem gwine stan
Colonizin in reverse"
—*Louise Bennett*

"We are more interested in the future than the past."
—*David Cameron*
on reparations for the transatlantic slave trade

After hearing Cameron on the radio
I dreamt of Uhuru Kenyatta refusing
to apologise for Africa's role in slavery
and under-developing Europe
because Africa is
more interested in the future.

I wake to say that even though I have come
to teach poetry, and not history,
our language has not come from the future,
it has crawled from a cave
and rowed to so many shores
that we speak in crashed waves and trade winds.

night 2

"The problem is not that we were once in charge [in Africa] but that we are not in charge any more."
—*Boris Johnson*

Dan, the Kenyan teacher, drives me to the airport
past Lake Victoria.
I ask him if he knows
the name of that lake
before 1858.
He says, *I could tell you*
but it has no meaning in English.

a year from home

hibaq osman

april

We were told the land had a whale's mouth
of ocean for each household,
free-flowing, unrestricted

I packed four necklaces that ward off evil,
Drooping eyelids, batteries
and bags of air in case I missed home

july

The school is a 'comprehensive'
My cousins say this is good,
the queen herself must know I am smart

bare lit anthology

august

There isn't as much water as we thought

With bare feet I walk a patch of grass
Above, the orb of flames
Burns insignia into my nape

november

I've shortened my words, y'know?
Sit at the sides of rooms and beg to be smaller,
My teachers don't look me in the eye

We don't have heavy tongues no more
I whisper my words into nooks and crannies
This is how the English are

february

Worship is different too,
There's no spirit to feel,
Only eyes at the back of my head

My great-aunt taught me how to sigh
She'd say: soft but deep, soft but deep
Or the ancestors won't hear you

In this land, they are all you have.

trading air

hibaq osman

Tonight,
you will hang your heart by your coat
and walk into my arms as if this was your only
      redemption
like a storm that has forgotten how to calm,
until your breathing slows
and my name is shoved between obscenities.
I have become familiar with hearing it like this
fast but slurred—
a secret forced to vacate your mouth.

I imagine you leave your shoes under my bed
because you are looking for reasons to stay
maybe one day I will clean them
and you will call this home.
Maybe I'll melt them in the oven,
make you walk barefoot on the damp concrete until

you find
another body to steal warmth from
but I am too busy counting your grip marks
to be bitter or better at love.

Tonight,
I will wear your coat and nothing else
dance before the heart you hung,
sigh into it
as if it were cascading water
daring you to get sick of me,
restless,
waiting
and all yours.

banjo on the motorway

tendai huchu

The summer I stopped bullshitting myself that I was a failed writer, I got my first real job in five years, doing removals with Adala Kojo. This, of course, is not to say writing is not a "real job," only it's one nobody in their right mind is willing to compensate (ideally an income commensurate to the labour expended, failing which, an acceptable pittance to keep body and soul together and maybe regularly purchase a few cans of super-strength lager) you for. Truth be told, given the huge gap in my CV and very little by way of practical skill in any field to fall back on, Kojo was the only person dumb enough or desperate enough to take me on.

It was a strange thing waking up before dawn, not with the muse or trying to tune into cosmic vibrations, but going through the routine motions of life in postindustrial UK. The rumble of Kojo's Luton van at four-thirty in the morning was calibrated to wake all the neighbours. I dashed out, piece of toast between my teeth, woollen hat on my bald head and a warm jacket over my shoulders. The van looked grey in the artificial lights, though it was actually white.

–Morning, boss, I said, opening the door and hopping onto the passenger seat.

Weren't nothing personal he didn't reply to me. Adala Kojo wasn't a morning person, and until the sun pissed warm yellow rays on his face, he was unlikely to say anything to anyone. Just nodded to the silver thermos on the dashboard and I helped myself to a cup of strong black coffee, mixed in with a few shots of Grant's. It burnt right through my oesophagus, warming my gut. The toddy was the only reason I made sure to eat first thing in the morning, however early we set out. On an empty stomach, it gave you the shits or made you want to fight the boss, both of which were unacceptable outcomes, given my fiscal circumstances.

–So where we going today?

It might seem crazy that I still asked him questions knowing full well he wasn't going to answer them, but it made me feel a bit more comfortable. There's that unnerving thing about hollowed-out silences when you're with another person, because you often find yourself wondering what they're thinking, and, if their thoughts are half as crazy as yours, then you'll do anything to disrupt them, to bring them back to reality, as it were.

Adala Kojo was a small, dark man, a Brit of Malawian origin via Zimbabwe. He was one of those older immigrant types who thought they were only coming over for a couple of years to make a quick buck and ended up staying longer than they ought to have. He had a large bald patch on top of his head and wispy, greying dreadlocks that grew on the sides and the back, which he tied into a ponytail. His beard grew in patches and tufts that made him look like a weasel. Eyes fixed on the road, he drove us through the wastelands of Doncaster, following the signs onto the A1, nose pointed up north.

I closed my eyes but didn't drift off to sleep. The on-coming headlights pierced my eyelids, creating red dots that glowed and faded into nothingness. I felt every bump on the road, the primeval roar of the ancient life-forms that powered our engine, and smelled the scent of Adala Kojo's Old Spice filling the cab of our van. That was the closest I ever got to dreaming those days. I was smoking too much and the herb had stolen my dreams, replacing them with heavy, deathlike slumber that brought little repose to the soul.

−Newcastle for our first pickup, then on to Ber-wick-upon-Tweed, said Adala Kojo finally, and I knew we'd been on the road about two hours. I've got the first shift, you can drive on the way down, cause I need to practice. That kosher?

−Whatever.

−Thanks, kid.

Kojo had a couple of us working for him on rotation. Mostly illegals and locals on the dole. He fell out with each of us in turn, sacked us all one at a time, but a few weeks later he'd come calling, everything right as rain again. It was cash-in-hand work. We received our remuneration in crisp portraits of the Queen, £60 per day for a porter, but if you had a licence, he gave you £85. I had a licence. This was completely under the table, no taxman. In the few actual conversations we had on the subject, Adala Kojo asserted what he was doing was no different to the activities of multinational corporations who paid armies of accountants and lawyers to shift their millions offshore (of course, with these guys' services there would be a legalistic transubstantiation from our tax evasion to perfectly lawful tax avoidance). Downside was Kojo didn't insure you on his Luton and that was the devil in the small print. But when you have nothing to lose—fuck it.

If you'd followed the motorways as long as we had, you ended up actually believing all of England was one continuous, hybrid-type conurbation as you were channelled through cities and towns, the little green taken up by monotonous farmland and industrial parks. You felt hemmed in by concrete and steel and glass and tar that choked your chi, and the only thing for it was to light a fag and turn your gaze to the sky. Grey clouds hung over everything, sucking up my blue smoke as it rose and went out the window.

We had a meal at the truck stop after Alnwick. Around East Linton, we got off at the services and both went to take a dump. For obvious reasons, we chose cubicles as far away from each other as possible, but having ridden together for so long, Adala Kojo and I had synchronised our bodily functions with uncanny precision. Naturally, it meant we took less stops along the way, saving time. The sooner the job got done, the sooner we got home.

—You ever think about taking up writing again? Kojo asked.

—Thought we agreed never to talk about that shit, I said.

—True, but oft times, what people say and what they mean are two different things.

—You still think you're gonna hit the big time, Adala? I threw the thing back in his face.

—The failure of a man is not in his falling down, but in his failure to rise up again, for if he stands again, he has not failed.

—Tell me one I haven't heard before, I said, rolling the window back up.

We dropped off the couch and box we'd picked up along the way to an address in Musselburgh and another in Leith, and drove through sunny Edinburgh to Cramond where we had our removals gig. The trick was to make sure the van was never empty, so Kojo picked up little jobs en route, making sure we (rather, he) maximised profit up and down the way. He did the logistics on anyvan.com, bidding for jobs against other couriers online, and if I'd had an ounce of ambition, I should have struck out on my own, but I was one of those guys that couldn't organise the proverbial piss-up in a brewery.

You could smell the money in Cramond, along with the salty sea air. We got to the semi on Whitehouse Road, just opposite the hotel. A middle-aged peroxide blonde, complete with pearl necklace, stepped out of the house to meet us. Her face was tight, worry-worn—we were used to this. A big move was enough to set anyone's nerves on edge. Truth be told, both Kojo and I fantasised that maybe one day the shit that happens in porn would happen to us. Lonely, rich housewife, horny as hell, wanting to be serviced D.P. by rough, anonymous tradespersons (NSA). The reality was a lot more mundane, though. You were lucky if you got a cup of tea. Usually, they (the lonely, rich housewives, horny as hell) were on your back trying to tell you how to do your fucking job—and they didn't tip either.

–You sure that van's big enough to take all our stuff? the lady said, before we'd even set foot on her river stone driveway.

–Mrs McTavish, what we have inside this rusty hunk of metal is one thousand cubic feet of space, and I can take three thousand kilograms too. I know I've gone both metric and imperial, that's because I've got enough room whichever way you choose to measure it, Kojo said, breaking out into a toothy grin. I could move the Queen, corgis and all, out of Buckingham and still have room to spare.

–Well, we're not paying any extra…

–No one's going to ask you to, ma'am. Let's just go through the inventory, and everything will be just fine.

The trick to loading a van is to make sure every cubic inch of space is utilised. First couch in, right side up, the next one upside-down, like fitting Lego. Pad everything and fill the holes with boxes and unpackable shit and stuffables, like cushions. Gaps are for saps. Then the square furniture, washing machines, fridges, all at the bottom, they can take the weight of the lighter, fragile stuff. My back was killing me. It started when we battled a vending machine in Basingstoke, and it never stopped since. Mattresses and the beds next. Remember to tie everything down with your ratchets. All it takes is a bit of common sense and working around Mrs McTavish who keeps trying to tell you what to do, though she hasn't a clue how the job is done. Smile and ignore.

When we were done, Adala Kojo went up to Mrs McTavish, made sure we'd collected everything, reached into his back pocket and gave her a colourful flier.

–What's this? she asked.

–See, I play a little and I have a gig tomorrow night. If you can make it that would be nice, he replied.

–A man of many talents, she said, and I could detect a hint of sarcasm. Doncaster is a little too far out for me, but thank you for the invitation.

–Ah, well, no problem. If you know anyone out that way please tell them to come to my show.

–I'll be sure to do that.

I turned to leave. Kojo was doing this thing with his fliers regardless of how far away from Donny we were. Twas almost like he actually believed our customers might actually come to see him jam. I felt sorry for the old fuck.

By the time I settled my ass behind the wheel, my T-shirt was soaked in sweat and my arms were aching, feet sore, and I remembered just how much I hated my job. We hit the A702, hoping to catch the M6, rolling Scottish countryside all around us, sheep and hills and not much else. Progress was slow, you'd hardly picked up speed before you hit the next curve. The alternative would have been to take the M8 towards Glasgow and then catch the M6 off that, but that would have added extra miles and extra fuel for our tank. I could see a tailback formed behind us in my mirrors, but what could I do about it? I shifted in my seat, trying to soothe my back. The GP had prescribed paracetamol, but it made me drowsy (a rare but well-documented side effect affecting roughly 2.82 percent of all users), so I couldn't take it on the road. After a while the pain would settle into a hot ache and maybe I'd have a little more toddy to see me through.

Kojo beside me opened and closed his mouth silently, singing a song, his hands strumming air guitar. Weren't no wild theatrical movements or anything fancy like that, just the methodical hand gestures of someone whose left knew the neck of a guitar and whose fingers on the right bore the callus marks of his passion. All I could hear from time to time was the occasional escape of air from his throat.

—Will you help me practice? he said.

—You still working on that song? What's it called?

—"Banjo on the Motorway."

—You gonna let me hear it now?

—No, but I need you to provide the beat. Can you go, pa-pum, pa, pa-pum, papa, pa-pum, pa?

He played imaginary drums to encourage me to pick it up. I knew the beat, we'd been jamming this track for near enough six months now. I gave it my best shot, and Adala Kojo silently strummed his air guitar like Carlos Santana while mouthing the lyrics to the song.

—Too fast, slow down, he said.

—It's a bit hard when I don't know what the damned song sounds like.

But I humoured him anyway. Adala Kojo never wrote the lyrics to his songs down. He created them in his head and edited them there. Said if a song weren't remembered, it weren't worth noting in the first place. Now, I don't know how many modifications "Banjo on the Motorway" had undergone, but I wondered how different this version was from the first conception of the track. A word redacted here and there. New line added. Slight change to the melody, maybe. I gave the old man the backing beat he needed and kept my eyes on the road. Southampton was far, far away.

I slept through most of Thursday, because it was late at night when we got back home. In the evening, I showered, dressed, and ate (in that particular order), and went to catch Adala Kojo's show. Vinnie's was a little dive tucked away on Wood Street, bang in the town centre. It had bright purple neon signs outside, complete with a lit-up martini glass and bikinied lady with huge tits that looked like something out of a grotesque modern art exhibition. The interior was firmly stuck in the eighties, though. Wooden wall panelling all round. A large crystal chandelier hung in the middle of the room. I sat in the booth nearest the small raised platform that served as the stage, behind which more tables and chairs were stacked. The place was virtually empty, save for two junkies drinking Strongbow and playing pool on the one table at the other end of the room. Thing is, I'd never seen Vinnie's packed. It always appeared teetering on its last legs, which explains the unsubstantiated rumours that Vincent Turner used the place to wash cash from other, more profitable enterprises of an unscrupulous nature.

Adala Kojo came in, guitar case on his back, and on either side he carried two big boxes. He wore Cuban heels that gave him an extra inch or two, bell bottoms from a bygone era, a crimson jacket, bowler hat covering his head, dreadlocks swinging loose, and dark sunglasses, as if his future was too bright to contemplate. I couldn't tell what dark emotions were hidden behind those shades as he surveyed the empty room, but he strode in with a strut, his wife and daughter trailing behind. I got up, greeted them all, asked what they wanted to drink and went to the bar at last.

The girl working the counter was called Cheryl, and she had that raven-goth vibe going on. We'd once got together, a one-night stand. I wanted more, she didn't, so clearly she was a girl with good taste. I got the maestro a double Jack (on the rocks), Carlsberg for me, and piña coladas for the girls.

–You think anyone's going to come? Kojo asked me, taking a sip out of the glass on whose rim the last punter had left a smudge of red lipstick.

–They'd be missing out if they didn't, I said. This gig's free, too, they have nothing to lose.

–I'm kinda nervous, you know.

–Just make sure you actually sing—none of that mime show you do in the van, you hear?

Kojo chuckled, and I left him setting up his synthesizer and guitar and went to join his family. A bunch of kids walked into the bar, scanned it, didn't like what they saw, and walked back out again. They couldn't have known they were missing out on a piece of living history. Adala Kojo had been lead guitar for Savannah Champagne, one of the hottest music groups to emerge from postindependence Zimbabwe. These guys were jamming at the same time as the Four Brothers, John Chibadura, Orchestra Murambinda Padhuze, and even the Bhundu Boys. They found some international fame and were even signed by Sony, but it all got to their heads, and in 1994 the band had split up. By 2015 Adala Kojo was the last surviving member of Savannah Champagne, his colleagues all dead from a cocktail of HIV/AIDS and poverty. He cut a lonely figure on the tiny stage, fiddling with his equipment, hooking up wires and pressing buttons. His movements were slow and deliberate; to me, he looked much older than he did during removals.

I sometimes wondered what he thought this gig would accomplish. Did he dream some exec from some record label would happen by this random bar in Doncaster on this random night and be so taken by the sound as to sign him on the spot? Would this be his huge comeback, the guy who once shared the stage with Madonna finally made good? I'd seen this stuff before on reality TV. Old pop acts and one-hit wonders from the past trying to resurrect their career on *X-Factor*, *The Voice*, *Pop Idol*, or, even worse, *Britain's Got Talent*. Inevitably, they got rejected, for these shows all wanted something young, fresh, new. This was no country for old men. It made me sad, and I felt my own years press on my weary joints.

Adala Kojo beckoned with his index finger and I went up to him.

–Doesn't look like anybody's coming, he said in a flat voice. I'll begin now.

–The show must go on, I said.

He tapped the microphone with his index finger, cleared his throat and introduced himself, more for the benefit of the two junkies than for the three of us who already knew him. Then he played his first song, "Rusununguko," one I knew from Savannah Champagne, though I'd never heard it in vocals other than Mike Batsirai's. Apparently Kojo wrote (dictated—his literacy skills were limited, a result of the segregated Rhodesian education system) most of the material on their first two albums. The music from the synth bounced off the walls of the empty room, caressed our beer glasses, and moved through the holes in our empty lives. The junkies applauded enthusiastically when he was done. He played a couple of tracks, veering from the Savannah Champagne catalogue and doing covers of Sting, Eric Clapton, and Jim Reeves, too.

Nearly half an hour in, the two junkies, both guys with sunk-in cheeks and large eyes, took to the dance floor. They had no rhythm, but they moved to the beat and that was all that mattered. Adala Kojo's missus got up, held out her hand, and soon it was the four of us on the dance floor, moving awkwardly in all the space around us, exposed to each other's sight, but Kojo's guitar kept us moving anyway. Cheryl took a bottle of Smirnoff and a couple of glasses and moved out from behind the bar onto the dance floor with us. She poured out free drinks, making the junkies leap with delight. And on the stage, I saw Kojo move like a demigod, his fingers working furiously to keep up with the prerecorded beats on the synthesizer, but jam he did. By God, he played.

After covering John Chibadura's "Mudiwa Janet," Adala Kojo announced he was giving us a taste of his brand new music. He told us matter of factly that we would be the first people in the world to hear it.

—I wrote this one on the road for you Elaine, my wife, love of my life, he crooned from the stage. You've been there for me through everything and this is my little way of saying thank you, because words alone will never be enough.

Adala Kojo paused and let us soak in the silence. He moved his right foot and kicked something on the synthesizer. It came: pa-pum, pa, pa-pum, papa, pa-pum, pa. And the first line of "Banjo on the Motorway" was a subtle killer, a landmine that lay hidden underground long after the war was over. Kojo leaned into the microphone, kissing it as he sang, and I knew, even with those dark shades on, that his eyes were closed and his heart was open. The words left his lips so delicately, straw bending in the rain (his two-decade-long immersion in the language made it infinitely superior to the awkward English tracks from his Savannah Champagne days), sorrow and joy, a love that was endless like the tarmac on the motorway. It wasn't a hit song. Far from it; it was the kind of tune you hear on the radio, wonder what it is, wait for the DJ to tell you, and they don't announce it, so it lingers in your head for a few more minutes, and then it disappears. Later on, you can't remember what the words were. The tune itself is lost to memory. You're desperate to know who sang it, all you recall is how it made you feel, but when you try to express this feeling, it is gone. And you never hear it again. That's what "Banjo on the Motorway" sounded like to me.

After the song finished, I walked out, caught a taxi, and went home to bed. It felt as though I had nothing left to stay for anymore. Damn his other tracks, "Banjo on the Motorway" had stabbed me through the left ventricle, and I needed to recover.

I don't know whether it's false memory or it truly happened, but I think I heard Kojo's van outside my house in the early hours of the morning. Maybe I heard knocking on the door or the doorbell ring. There were several missed calls on my phone, all from Adala Kojo. We were meant to do a house move in Sheffield, and I'd fucked up. My head was heavy, and I was hungover from the vodka.

It was only around midday that Elaine called me. Adala Kojo and Desmond Mambi had been sideswiped by an Eddie Stobart truck just as they were coming onto the M40. Kojo was killed straight away (a lot of thoughts went through my mind (If I had woken up when I was supposed to and gone with him, the accident wouldn't have happened because he'd have been on the road earlier, without having to go to Desmond's, therefore he wouldn't have met the truck (or maybe I would have been in there with him)), none of which could ever change the circumstances), and Desmond was critical at the Royal Hallamshire. Elaine's voice was cold; maybe she was blaming me too. I couldn't tell then and I don't know now. I offered to go to her place, but she refused and said she'd inform me of when the funeral would be.

I got off the phone and sat up in bed, my head still pounding. It didn't feel like a dream because sometimes reality is so heavy you feel its weight on your entire being. Just yesterday. No, hours. A few hours ago. It made no sense, and that is what made it true. And I thought to myself, I once knew a man who could write a song in his head. One day I too would write a story about that man in my head, carry it for months, memorise every line, erase some, edit it, and when it was ready I would sing it like a tree falling in a forest in a dingy dive in Doncaster.

gannet

vera chok

*She saw it. A tattoo on a thigh showed through really thick
tights. "Founder" it seemed to read. Founder? It's not right but
she doesn't— She sees scissors, sharp. Hears (feels) nylon giving
in. High up the thigh, facing nowhere in particular. "Founder" in
cheap cursive. Thinks, Who else knows?*

*She flicks her gaze up. It lands on the woman's mascaraed lashes,
finely done. The face around them's a landscape of paleness. Is she
dreaming of steamed eggs, miso soup, fingers dipped in salt?*

*The train rattles and grinds. An arrival. Whose departure? At
the last possible moment, she stands, leaves, walks up the escalator.*

I watch her sidestep through the perfectly wide open
door and I promise myself: stick to the plan of morning
stretches daily, hot yoga once weekly, push-ups whenever I walk past my stairs. I want to feel strong. I want better shoulders. I choose life. But Julia, poor Ju. She wants

vera chok

Sorry I'm late! Let me just—oof!—grab a coffee and I'll be right with you.

That day we were in Brighton. God, I've hated that place since. The sky's so blue, she piped. Like a jerk, I shot her a glance. Cut her down, laughing. Where is it funny? Where do I think it's funny, exactly?

It is *blue!*

Julia loves the word "periwinkle" because:
    (a) The phrase "periwinkle blue" had once come out of John Malkovich's mouth
    (b) It referred to both a flower and a mollusc
    (c) Doesn't it sound just a little bit naughty?
She practically lit up if the word approached her mind.

She wants

It's a miracle we've got a table. I mean, how did you get us a table? Oh darling, it's so lovely to see you again.

That's ok. It's ok, darling. Darling, I've flung a thousand, million tiny hooks in your direction. Slinting, testing air like tongues. Travelling through time never did make it easy.

Gavin up a ladder. We gawped from a distance, nice sixth formers in skirts (mine ripped). He was a trainee fireman, yes, really, and in his spare time, he fixed things up at the school. How in God's name had that been approved? Tousled-haired Gavin with trainee fireman's arms. Four hundred girls under one roof. You might as well have, no, let's not go there. Julia was oblivious. I was disgruntled. Back in my room, Karen practiced flirting on me while Ju jabbered on about ponies and crumpets or whatever it was she was into at the time.

I did not like being practiced on. Karen made everything sound filthy. Blood rushed to my face, teenager that I was. I shoved her away, inasmuch as I dared to touch her, and shot Ju a look. Ju was stuffing her face with toast. Recently arrived from tropical climes smack bang into our lovely English winter, she'd promptly lost her skinny, pretty, sports-girl looks via loaves of bread, toasted and buttered, dripping. She detested the idea of chilly air anywhere near her skin and refused to do games especially because it meant stripping in front of us pale, goosepimpled chickadees. I bet she had lovely skin. I'll train in the summer when it's warm, she used to say, licking her salty lips. A trap. For crumbs. I saw it.

Julia grew, wrapped up in moist, white bread. Grew folded into saltbutter warmth. I wanted to slap her out of it. I saw oil stains in the carpet. She chowed down on soggy slices and waited for the next pair to brown. To stave off the cold, she rampaged through loaves, ate bowls of custard, finished food off our plates. Gannet, we joked. Gannet! She didn't know what that was. She didn't know what "a ham" looked like either. Years later when she was working in a country hotel during the holidays, they sent her to the pantry to fetch "the ham." Julia, familiar with pink slices of meat in a packet, didn't recognise the shapeless hunk on the shelf. Where is it funny? *Mango. Do you know what* that *looks like? Ha ha ha.* They'd fancied themselves as a modern British sort of place. A boy of nine, Ollie, washed the pots. English. Surprising. He wanted the cash just as she wanted the cash. I guess that made it all right. A boy from uni rang her mobile nightly and had no idea of the cost. Professed he didn't care. They laughed into the night. Ha. Ha.

Ha.

Julia knows mangoes though, newspaper-wrapped and hanging like heads. Her mum up a ladder, stapler in hand, wrapping each hard, green item in paper to ward off pests. Ju would hand up sheet after sheet, looking like a village boy from spending too long in the sun. Are you Malay? Taxi drivers would ask. *No, no, not Malay.* Holidays at the beach, you see. Mum's brother's company beach bungalow share. They would drive down, both families, excited dachshund nose-printing the windows, gasping to catch the first glimpse of brown waves. She'd bathe looking out to sea, eat neat chicken sandwiches with the crusts cut off, spend hours taunting her little cousins with made-up games. Middle class as you like, if you like. Only this wasn't England so this wasn't class. Oh, aspirations.

All of us want

She remembers mangoes, yes. Crying out and leaping, crunching ant bodies under the tree. Large red bodies hard to kill, raining down and into her clothes. They liked mangoes too. But ham. Here ham was unclean.

In the picturesque village hotel in Oxfordshire, no one ever asked her for directions. In the city, they shout her shoulders in. Where is it funny?

Julia

I watch her sidestep   wants
                  The train grinds
                  The thigh shifts
                  The tattoo is   *toast*

the nod

jennifer nansubuga makumbi

One thing you must understand from the onset is that out here in Britain, there is an idea, something felt, of being one, of 'we're in this together' among black folks, call it the black nation for want of a better term. At times it can feel tighter than tribes (in an African sense); sometimes it is as intense as religion. In fact, out here, some people will call you 'sister' or 'brother' the way people back home do in churches. Within the nation there are certain expectations and understandings, not imposed but understood. When strangers share experiences, they're amazed at how similar their sensibilities are regardless whether they come from the islands, from the continent, or from the Americas. One of the outward manifestations of the nation is the nod.

Now, when I arrived at this party the guests were so natural around me I forgot myself. I forgot myself because I did not see myself in their eyes. It is true we see ourselves in the eyes of others. I did not realise this until I came to Britain. When they look at you, people's eyes are mirrors. The problem is, eyes are constant mirrors, and you are always looking at yourself.

But as I said, on this occasion, I was simply not there in the guests' eyes, and so I did not look around to see how many others like me were at the party. That is the other thing. Out here, when you are different, especially when you've just come from your home country, when you arrive at an unfamiliar place or an event your eyes can't help scanning the guests, the crowd, the seminar group for someone like you or for the nation. Actually, we do it on the road too. It is reflex. I guess we do it because there is warmth in numbers. There is also the assurance that since there are others like you, then your way of being, your behaviour on that occasion, will not carry the burden of being the reference for all your kind's way of being.

Once you have identified someone, you wait to catch their eye. In most cases when you do, you smile or nod. Sometimes, however, you catch an eye that panics, *oh no, not one of you*, or another that flashes, *fuck off*. Some folks will avoid catching your eye intentionally and stay well clear of you. But in most cases, there is a flicker, an acknowledgement of, *I am glad you're here too*. Someone gave it a name, it is called the nod. But as I said earlier, when I arrived at this party I was made so comfortable I did not look around for the nation. And that is when things went wrong. See, I didn't see her; I didn't give her the nod.

Looking back now, I suspect that even if I had seen her I might have not identified her. I think she saw me arrive, tried to catch my eye, but I glanced past her. She must have thought I was one of those fuck-off types. And in terms of slights within the nation, that is one of the worst. Unfortunately for me, she was not the kind of sista you blanked and got away with it.

The party was in one of those rich areas where children stop playing and stare as you walk past. And if you catch them at it, they smile, "hello." Nothing rude, just that they don't see people like you often. Even though I had just arrived in the country and everywhere England looked the same to me (I mean, houses on a street tend to look similar because builders in this country are so lazy, at so many levels, it's not even funny), I could tell that this was an exclusive area from the distances the houses shrunk from the road. Such large compounds you could build a second house. Hedges grew untamed. (In poor areas, hedges are clipped to diminutive heights; you let your hedge grow high, your neighbours complain to the council that it blocks the sun.) Along the way, I came to parts of the village where the woods were so dense it felt like walking in a forest. That's how wealthy this place was.

When I arrived, Annabelle's family were waiting. You would think I was a long lost cousin. Everyone knew my name: everyone had been waiting. "Let me take your coat, Lucky…did you have a good journey on the train… Cup of tea, Lucky: Autumn it's getting nippy…ah, British weather: it must be awful for you…Red or white wine…Try this cake, Lucky…oh, I love your dress… you didn't get lost, did you…we were worried…"

But this growing up in Uganda, I tell you: it can be treacherous in Britain. Now me, I was brought up with the notion that as a visitor it's rude to say no to food, especially when someone brings it to you. So I accepted everything the women brought to me and they gave me a lot, "try this, Lucky…you're gonna love this meringue cake…piece of lasagne…that is quiche…this is elder-flower, you must try it…" In the end, there were plates and plates and glasses around me. Don't misunderstand me, it was mostly new food and I was eager to try it all, but I was worried that the numerous plates made me look gluttonous. This is why Ugandans in Britain will tell you that the British did not give your culture the visa: leave it at home.

Then Annabelle came to my rescue, "Oh my God, Lucky, they're gonna feed you to death. Here"—she picked up the plates—"come with me"—she walked me to the kitchen. "Put all that food away and get yourself something you *really* want to eat." She dumped the food on work surfaces and walked back to the garden, where her engagement party was held. But me, I was still too Ugandan. As soon as she left the kitchen, I poured the food away in the bin. Yes, wasting food is abominable, but no way was I going to leave my rudeness displayed like that! What if the people who served it to me saw that I had rejected their food?

I was reaching for the chocolate cake when a voice from behind me said, "You have such lovely skin."

I glanced at her, smiled, "Thank you," and turned back to the chocolate cake.

"It must be all that sun in Africa: the weather in this country is not right for *our* skin."

"Yes," I agreed without looking at her. My eyes were so focused on the delicate job of balancing a slice of cake on a spatula towards my plate that I did not register the words, *our skin*. In fact, when my slice was safe on the plate, I added, "My grandmother says that sweat is the best moisturiser," to reinforce the notion that the sun in Africa was really good for the skin.

Truth be told, that was a lie. It was not my grandmother, it was my mother. My mother is what they call New Age in Britain. But the word 'grandmother' gave it a *je ne sais quoi*, let's call it the weight of African wisdom. It is something I turn on sometimes in Britain, especially when among the nation, to play up on the difference, you know, African age-old wisdom (often common sense) versus western research (the silly ones). Truth is, my grandmother is a city girl. She swears by Yardley products—soaps, talcum powder, deodorant, and perfume. When she strays from Yardley, she goes to Avon. She would be seriously offended if she found out that I had appropriated what she calls my mother's madness to her.

Then I heard the woman's *our skin* and stopped. That phrase came straight out of the nation. That's where we say *our* this, *our* that. I looked at her properly. My mind was frantic, *is she a Zimbabwean, South African, or Namibian white?* That's where my mind goes when I meet white Africans in Britain. But white Africans would never say 'our skin.' They'll say 'our weather,' 'our economies,' 'our politics,' never 'our skins.' What I did not realise was that she could see every wave of my frantic thoughts in my eyes as I tried to place her. Then I began to see traces of the sub-Sahara in her: it had been there all along if I had I looked past the skin. Then I saw the anger. The, *how dare you search for my blackness*, the, *so I am not black enough!* In that moment, when I realised that she had seen my realisation, we spoke with just the eyes—hers fiery with injured indignation, mine withering with mortification—until she relented and the glare in the eyes flickered to a shade of, *okay, I'll let you off this time* and smiled, "Really," in response to my grandmother's wisdom, as if her eyes had not been haranguing me.

I flashed a sista smile (I was wont to overdo the camaraderie now). "Well, sweat is nature's moisturiser, people don't realise. It has perfect pH and it moisturises the skin from within, softening both layers. These creams we buy only work on the surface: they don't even penetrate the top layer. Our skin needs to sweat regularly." I had turned on the conspiratorial tone we use in the nation when we discuss food (don't eat anything out of a tin, cook from fresh), health (watch out; we put on a lot of weight in winter. Take vitamin D supplements for the bones. Go home to the islands or the continent at least once a year to get proper sunshine and eat proper food to rejuvenate the body. For some reason weight drops off when we go home, no matter how much we eat), and products specific to our bodies (skin, hair, or jeans that fit our thighs but don't betray our butts when we sit down and fit around the waists at the same time).

"I go to sauna four days a week and drink a lot of water just to sweat. When I step out my skin is really soft to touch. Besides, I've not yet found the right moisturiser. I use Vaseline."

That was true at the time. For some reason, the air in Britain made my skin so dry, moisturisers marked 'for very dry skin' lasted only a few minutes and my skin would be dry again. The hands were desiccated, I swear. I resorted to applying cream, waiting a few minutes, applying again, and then using Vaseline Petroleum Jelly to lock it in. It took me a while to discover the ethnic beauty shops in Hulme, which had appropriate creams. I thus expected her to step in and recommend a few moisturisers. She did not. Instead, she reached for the chocolate cake, cut a piece, turned around, and leaned against the work surface. I waited as she bit into the cake because I could see she was about to say something. I dared not interrupt, not after my faux pas.

"I've always wondered which one of my parents was black."

I put my cake down. Now she had me by the scruff of my neck. The thing about the nation's sensibilities is that sometimes you can take blackness too seriously and it can be pretty heavy to carry. Like black guilt. Knife crime in London. In that moment, I was at once African, Caribbean, and African American men who had travelled to Britain and had children but, for whatever reasons, did not bring them up. Don't ask why men. Black guilt was screaming 'absent fathers.' What could I say to her? I concentrated on looking guilty.

"I am now sure my father was African, a student. He was from either Liberia or Sierra Leone, though now I know that he could have been a coloured from South Africa because, obviously, I am too pale." There was accusation in 'obviously'—*obviously you did not notice me*—and emphasis on 'too pale' as in *too pale to be black*.

Something, I don't know what, made me say, "Some Africans, especially in Zimbabwe and other Southern African countries, can be really pale."

Her eyes flashed, *don't correct me*, but she carried on, "He finished his studies and returned to Africa. At the time, Africans that came to Britain were students and could not wait to go back to their countries after their courses. My mother was young, adventurous, and no doubt Irish. He didn't realise she was pregnant when he left. And she did not know his address in Africa."

I imagined her as a child. Lying in bed constructing her family. She began with the father and made him black. Then her mother, who she made white. She constructed the circumstances of her birth and how she ended up wherever she was at the time. But as she grew older and more knowledgeable, she was forced to change things, make specific adjustments to her parents in order to fit what she looked like and the time of her birth. I was confident that at one time her father had been Caribbean complete with an island; he had also been African American with a state and an accent. However, she had now settled on Africa, and she was not going to be moved.

"Teta is a Liberian name."

"Oh!" I was put straight. Africa was guilty. I smiled, "What a lovely name!" It was the first thing that came to mind. Then I regretted it. Why was everything that came out of my mouth either woefully inadequate or patronising? I should have said, *Nice to meet you, Teta: my name is Lucky* and shaken her hand.

"It was the fifties," she went on. "In them days, more Irish women had relationships with black men. But she was young and could not bring up a child on her own. She gave me up for adoption."

The fifties were like a rope thrown to me. I clung onto it: "You don't look like you were born in the fifties," I said. And it was true. She did not look a year older than forty. "Honestly, I thought you were in your thirties."

"Oh, you're so kind."

But Teta was not interested in looking young. She had found me, I had blanked her, then I dared to search her body for her blackness, I was African, I was going to pay for her abandonment as well.

"If you look at my wedding pictures, there are no black people. My husband is Italian and comes from a large family. There were so many people at the wedding, people imagined it was both our families. But of course deep down they were asking, where are her black folks?"

"It's your moment, Teta!"

I did not see Brenda, Annabelle's mother, come in. She grabbed Teta's hand and steered her towards the door. "Wait till you hear Teta sing," Brenda winked at me.

There was something about the way Brenda led Teta away: as if I was not the first person she had rescued

99

from her. Yet the fact that she was going to sing at this party made me uncomfortable. I tell you, being in Britain can make you hypersensitive. Or maybe it is the nation's sensibilities. It is easy to give offence out here and even easier take it. For some reason, it seemed a cliché to me that Teta was going to sing: as if it was to perform her blackness. I am black, I can sing. But Teta was not done with me, oh no! As they got to the door, she looked back and asked, "You're Lucky, aren't you?"

I knew she was not asking about my name: Teta was too sneaky for that. She was accusing me of being lucky—lucky that I knew where I came from, lucky that I knew my parents, lucky that I was so privileged in my blackness that I had questioned hers. She saw that I understood what she was doing and smiled, "Lovely name," and stepped out.

"The Bitch."

In that moment I was aware of being alone in Annabelle's house. There was such silence I heard the house being outraged. The corridor stared, mouth open. The kitchen, its appliances, the food, everything acted like they were the nation. I pushed the cake away, sucked my teeth deep and prolonged, African style, and hurried out.

I sat at the back and watched Teta sing "Havah Nagilah." There were no traces of the earlier confrontation on her face whatsoever. She never looked at me again. I wondered whether she was one of those floating souls who once in a while made a landing. That day she had anchored on me, rattled me, and took flight again. Annabelle saw me sitting alone and came. "What are you doing hiding at the back, Lucky? Come sit with us."

I smiled. She was blissfully unaware of the nation at her party. If I had explained what had transpired between me and Teta, she would have perhaps thought it a storm in teacup.

trash

selma dabbagh

It seems the pattern is that you arrive with heavy-bot-tomed bottles and leave me sprinkled with the oiled corners of condom packets. You take the bottle (now empty) and the other trash connected to your visit and this is *kind*—I guess—although I know it is also because it is *evidence* of what happens. What happens being the filling of me, causing a stillness so complete that sometimes I feel I was a puppet who had become frazzled in my wires and you made them into lace, or silk, as I am laid calm in my lace & silk & messy with you. And we get to the place where you ask me to tell you of all the times when I felt *you* before you were there and the many times when I wished for *you* and you weren't. Like earlier when I was held for hours trying to get out of the airport and I felt you quieting me. They were going through my equipment + I thought it's ok, it's ok, because I was on my way to you. And then there's the silly stuff you are so anxious to know about, like when I was 24 + in a room in Alexandria + there was the sea + I was studying lying on the bed (why did you ask about the bedcover?) + the window was open a bit + I lay there with dreams of a knuckled hand on my hip bone—a grasp of desire—which I can only describe as being *you* and all the decisions and choices I've taken to lead me to where I am, that I can only say were because I one day wanted to explain them to *you*. *You* were there when I dreamt of kisses and fairy-tale princes. *You* were also there in the US Army bar in Baghdad when the man, the soldier with the bicepts (I can't spell, sorry, I'm still a bit whirring and buzzed, it never was my thing I was always a *do-er*) and small, reckless eyes leant for me not at all scared of the face that I have, that I have had to professionally train to be angular (so angular now I feel I am nothing but a skull growing on a stick) and prim, to portray competence, reliability + trust to be UTTERLY UNAPPROACHABLE because there shouldn't be a single *asshole* out there who watches the news who hasn't seen my perfected mug beamed into their space on their screen, but that *asshole* had the AUDACITY to lean in at me going on about my *skinny ass* & they laughed, the group. Why he got to me I don't know, but I'd just come back from the South and had the stink of bodies + gas in my nose and the grab, grinding rush of flying over dust roads in a jeep with a tag car + a lead + even then you know I felt *you* were there.

And today you were really there—*here*—but I didn't want to tell you about the cameraman who they've been going for, saying he's Intelligence and I'm now the most senior (I'm not circus master, but hey I'm close) + it's now my show y'know that I'm resp'b to get him out of there—but here we were, with my phone blipping away on the desk with like a gazillion calls, texts + emails from London, Washington, NY, Head Office blipping through + I just had to say *what the fuck?* You know, I needed you, because hey you might come with a dark bottle of bubbly + I can glam the whole thing up and you can turn me into lace-stringed limp loveliness and transform me back into a *girl* in this hotel room, so I don't have to cope will all the shit going on out there which was *insane* today btw if you haven't seen the news, but I needed you and I knew it would just be a couple of hours, because then you are back home with your XXXX, which is *you know*, the *deal* which I took on board from the outset + that's *cool* except it's hard when I see you like the line of constant running through my life + when you are so intent on knowing every part of it + I feel sometimes that it was easier when you existed in my life before I ever knew you.

aya

sharmila chauhan

My husbands say I am beautiful. As I watch them from my bedroom window, their shadows meld together under the frangipani tree. Sem sits on the ground watching the moon, one side of his face tinged with silver. Next to him, Jerome and Omar smoke their bheedis. The tobacco-filled flutes are as long and slender as their fingers. They will sit there until the moon is high and the sky twinkles like a queen's anklet. Now and then they talk. Voices low, their backs to me, words pass between them, shrouded like cards.

The breeze is light but heady. Filled with the promise of a cool and comfortable night. The air sinks gently into the basin, collecting every nub of fragrance, from the jacaranda trees to the tiny unopened jasmine buds. It climbs gently up the hill, into my room, filling me with longing.

On the dawn of my wedding day, I slipped jasmine under my breasts. That night I watched Shai's eyes fill with desire as he undid my blouse. I kissed him and then, laughing, we fell onto the bed, crushing the flowers with our bodies.

I'd met Shai when we were sixteen. We were married before my seventeenth birthday. People said we were too young, that I should have waited for my husband to acquire some skills besides flute playing and simple harvesting. That I, in my headstrong nature, would eventually despise the mischievous, somewhat cavalier personality of my husband. It was true: I was young and he foolish. But we grew together, leaning on the other for support, always rising together towards the sun.

At that time our community was still young. I was the second generation born here, but the plight of our sisters Outside still weighed heavily on us. Battered and raped women would often come to the gates to find shelter. While seeing to their wounds, my mother often spoke of the chronic infanticide and feticide that left few women in India. Polyandry had become the norm, both in our community and Outside. Yet Outside was the worst type of servitude, with both physical and sexual degradation. We were lucky, the Elders told us—born into a community that not only valued women, but had returned to the old traditions. Finally Woman had found her rightful place, and the results were clear: children were educated, everyone found work, and there was relative harmony. There is a saying here, "In the place where there was drought, now grows rice. In the place where women were subjugated, there is now growth and freedom."

It was in our custom that I, as the eldest daughter, would bring my husband home to my family. I did as was expected. My mother had a busy home with four daughters and twelve husbands. The house was filled with activity from dusk until midnight, and it was seldom that we were alone. Our lovemaking suffered. Shai was often tired or had tasks to finish before bed. He claimed that I wore him out; that he had to work the next day; that I didn't understand how much he had to do. I laughed and cajoled him, sometimes he relented, but this wasn't what I wanted for marriage. We were irritable and argued often, and in public.

My mother worried that I didn't conceive quickly. She even suggested, as is our custom if a man is infertile, that I take another husband. But I didn't want to marry another man. I only wanted one. After six months, I decided to renovate a small house on the hill. We left my mother's house and moved there just after summer. My sisters were angry, the other women in the village envious. They said we were wrong and selfish. We didn't care.

We came alive on the golden hill, we grew our own food. We did it all together, he raking, I sowing. He chopping, I cooking. Afterwards, we would never be too tired to talk or make love. For seventeen summers we watched the harvest and the weaving of the silks in the square. We planted a frangipani tree in our courtyard, and when it bloomed, the young girls climbed up the hill to pick the flowers. It was said they were the sweetest of all. We gave them baskets to take as much as they wanted. We were already full of its scent and love.

Then, one morning, Shai didn't wake up. Not even when the midday sun washed over his face in a haze of almond white. When I touched his skin it was burning with fever, and his eyes were dark as if the oceans were churning inside. When the Healer arrived I could tell she smelt something rancid. Yet she smiled, closed the door, and told me to pray and fast. I did. For seventeen nights and days, I ate nothing but figs and water.

On the eighteenth morning, she told me I could go in. The room smelt damp and musty, even though the windows were open and the breeze high in the ceiling. My Shai was emaciated. His skin dry and grey as if moth-eaten. His beautiful eyes were sunken, yet his smile was arresting. We did not speak. Instead, I pressed my hand on his heart and wrapped him into my arms. We stayed like that until dusk. Until his hands were cold.

I went to his parents' house. His mother had made the funeral arrangements. I saw Sem. He had been only a boy when I'd married his brother Shai. On the eve of the cremation, Sem turned sixteen. After the ceremonies, as tradition dictated, I brought him to my home, to his brother's bed.

So Sem came to me as a boy, on the cusp of his manhood; a softer, more malleable version of his brother. The same warm, dark skin; eyes that shone when squeezed into a smile. Yet the disparity between them was heartbreaking. Where Shai's very nature had been light and carefree, Sem was heavy and morose. He was lost, and the air inside him was damp and blue.

It is said that the union between a woman and her new husband must take place within seven nights of the funeral. I admit that I took Sem with trepidation. He was stiff and afraid, but I was gentle and guided him as I knew I must. Yet it was difficult, an endurance for us both. There were times when, lying on top of him, a flash of his eyes or the turn of his cheek brought his brother back to me. After the seven nights, I could do no more.

Despite this, Sem was considerate and kind. The sorrow of our loss drew us together like two shells on the shore. Mornings, he went to the fields, doing the work of two people. Slowly I began to wait for him. Sometimes I even cooked. On Fridays we would drink and talk, our laughter echoing between the kitchen walls, long after the sun had gone down. Sometimes when I asked, Sem would bow his head and follow me to my room.

Afterwards, I would cry for Shai, for the betrayal. When each month the blood came, ruby red, sparkling with emptiness, I was glad. But I knew that Sem deserved more than the desperate attempts of a grieving widow.

Grief clings like an army of bush ants. As I peeled one off, the next clung on with a tighter grip. On the anniversary of Shai's passing, I couldn't get out of bed, eat, wash, or even talk. Within days I was skin and bones. My bowels quivered continuously, but my stomach became swollen like a hard ball. Sem called my mother; after all, a man knows little of such things. I could feel Shai closer than my breath. Sem was afraid, but he knew me better than I thought. One morning while my mother had gone to check the fields, he came to my room bearing a cup of warm honey water. It was a drink Shai used to make for me. How he even knew, I do not know. He made me sit up and lifted off the beaded cover. By then Sem was much taller and stockier than his brother, and as I leaned into his chest, I felt a strength from his presence. He held my head and made me drink. The storm passed. My insides opened as the honey glided down my throat and into my chest. I felt calm, the sugar mixing with my sorrow, producing the alchemy of surrender.

Later he brought him to me—Jerome, the man who'd given him the honey. The ferenghi from the west. His skin bruised by our sun, his jaw soft with age. When I saw him, something changed inside me. I wanted him. I looked into Sem's innocent face, and my heart ached. Could he have known? Known that I would take this stranger into our house, that I would take him to my bed? Give him my body, my pains, so he could suck them out of me?

Jerome was training to be a Healer. I listened as he told me how he'd traveled from the cool alpine forests to find the secrets in ours. And then I yielded, simply and as easily as crumbling red earth, parched from the heat. We spent many evenings reading together and debating. And truth be told, I wasn't often in the company of such a well-read man. During the day, he roamed the fields searching for herbs and flowers. I didn't miss him much, yet when he returned, I was always pleased.

The seasons changed, and on the anniversary of Shai's death, Jerome told me he would try to cure me. I was still a young woman then, my breasts high on my chest, my hips round and ripe. I wanted to live and love again. That night he gave me something to drink, and as I groaned he made me talk. Talk until the acid filled my mouth and I vomited. Then he looked around the room, taking hold of the shadows, dancing with each one until it fell to the ground and disappeared.

I don't know what Jerome did or what he had seen. But I felt calmer, more grounded in my body. The stream of emotions had dulled, and there was clarity. But also fear. This man, this foreigner, was clearing my soul of Shai. This was not our way.

I left shortly after that, leaving Sem and Jerome. Our community has an informal relationship with a coastal village. There, our men and women mix with the rest of the world. There, the world continues its ways, with its many stories of raping and kidnapping. But it is an amazing place with a pale blue sea and finely powdered sands. Foreigners with their pale, red skin and sparse clothing paraded up and down the coastline. The town is old, full of people weaving in and out of winding streets. The transience startled me at first, but then became irresistible in its energy.

The women of the coast are suspicious; they veil themselves and protect their beauty from the elements. I fell in love with them. Years of mixing with their colonial masters and Eastern traders had brought much to their looks. Their hair was thick, their noses strong and long. Embers of henna, burnt crimson lines on their palms, and their bangles played harmonies to their every move. I enjoyed watching them congregate at the harbour and spent much time there.

Omar had a boat. He too stood by the docks, but he was looking for work. Usually a lone foreign tourist searching for adventure, and a little heat. I'd seen him and the others like him, their skin deep copper, their bodies shapely and young. Their dhotis wrapped low around their waists, inviting eyes to proceed downwards. I didn't blame them. After all, there is a need for their services. Omar was older, his hair long and plaited. Waist thickened a little, yet he wore his dhotis as low as the others, as if to say he didn't care. He waved at me often, sometimes taking breakfast at the adjacent table; he knew better than to invite himself. Over a few days, we struck up conversation. He was well versed in local traditions, and since I had never visited the area before I let him take me on long walks through the markets. There were many things to be seen—crabs crawling over one another in small buckets and powdered seaweed for beautification. In an alleyway, he stopped and showed me large pink pig ovaries. They're used as a contraceptive, he told me. I raised my eyebrows, surprised to see them sold so boldly. In our community such manipulation is illegal and children, girls especially, vital. But the coastal women were brazen. I supposed their difficult lives made it necessary. Maybe the women at the coast are not powerful, Omar whispered, but they take their power another way. He grinned. At that moment I took his hand. We were together after that.

At first I wasn't sure of how much to give. I placed some notes in his hand the first night, but he shook his head. That wasn't how it was done, he said, pushing me onto the bed. I was simply to pay for food and give him gifts when he asked for them. But when after several days Omar stayed by my side day and night, not asking for a rupee, I didn't know what to think. I loved his company—the easy way with which he carried himself, his long plait swinging on his back. During the day he would fish or go out on his boat. Sometimes I would go with him, dangling my hands in the water as we passed through the mangroves. Sometimes he would stop, unwrap his dhoti, and drop the anchor. Our lovemaking was steady and passionate. Often I took him several times a night, laughing when his exhausted groan could not contain the excitement between his legs. I enjoyed him thoroughly.

Yet after the third week, the town began to suffocate me. The tiny streets, the gossip and heat. Even the sea breeze couldn't cool my senses. My melancholy had returned in its usual resolute and unshifting way. I began preparing for the trip home. On the day of my departure, Omar arrived with a small bag and some tools. He told me he was coming too.

The journey home took several days. During this time I found my peace. *With Omar things could change.* The only ache in my heart was for Sem. For his face when he would see Omar. I knew it would hurt him, and I promised myself to pay him more attention.

For a while it worked. True, Sem's face darkened when he saw Omar, but his spirits soon lifted when, on the second night, I called for him. He was eager as a puppy and I was able, for the first time, to take pleasure in our union. Something had changed. Very soon, Shai became a sweet, buried memory, and it was good for all of us. Slowly the men began to know each other. Sem was good in the fields, tending plants and harvesting. Jerome cooked, and Omar did the work around the house. It was harmonious. Unlike in many households, the men never bickered or picked childish disagreements. I was pleased when they went off on walks together to town or even when they took a trip to the coast to bring back some fresh fish and crab.

Finally I felt free. Free to admit I was no different to the other women. That I was no longer tied to the notion of one man, one love. It was so exhilarating that sometimes I even wondered whether Shai had been a mistake.

At night I took one of them to my bed; love was easy and plentiful. But I was always careful to avoid the times around the half moon when I was most fertile. If they noticed, they never said anything. My mother was the only dark cloud, and she warned me about bringing not one, but two, foreigners into the community. She said they would rebel and bring me misery. I told her she didn't know my husbands, that she didn't know me.

When autumn came we celebrated the Harvest Festival as a family. The men were each given a necklace. Sem's was the thickest, as he was the only "true" husband of the household. Both Omar and Jerome received thinner, though not meager, chains. That night there was an argument and then a few days of sulking and grumbling. Finally I sent them away to the coast, hoping time together would ease the matter.

When they returned, things changed. Meals would be late or the animals were left hungry. The house repairs fell behind. Their weekly visits to the market became more frequent. After dinner, they took to sitting together under the tree. When I had signaled for one to come to my room, he would take his time, telling me there was still work to be done. Sometimes I would get so tired I would fall asleep waiting. In the morning, I would hear them laughing in the kitchen, but by the time I went downstairs they were gone.

In my hours alone, I began to see Shai again. Smiling at me as I came out of the bath, picking a stray hair from my face when I was reading. I still ached for him. But there was nothing to be done. My mother came and looked with dismay. She told me that I must see the doctor and find out why I hadn't conceived. I couldn't tell her that I did not want a child. That, even with Shai, I had always avoided it. Just through my thoughts I was betraying her and my community. She told me that if none of my husbands could father a child, I would have to take another.

One night, I heard heavy footsteps at the door. Omar was drunk. There was a half moon behind him. He knew. Of all of them, it was Omar who would do it. But I didn't want Omar's seed. Not a thing from passion and girlish lust. Not into my virgin womb. He took me hard and fast, only taking pleasure for himself. After he left, I washed lemon inside myself and prayed. But Jerome was there the next night, and so it began.

I hardly see Sem anymore. The other two always come instead, waiting by my door, with easy confidences. When I spoke to Sem about it, he hung his head and was silent. When I looked closer I saw a tear run down his cheek. But he seems so at ease, so comfortable with them, it is difficult to know what to think. He knows that I suffer. He must, as the blood of his brother runs through him.

Perhaps they are afraid—afraid that my empty womb means another husband is on his way. Yesterday Sem asked me if the rumours were true. I told him yes, there is a man, from the village this time. He is a widower too, so perhaps we will share something. My mother had arranged the match, and truth be told I found little reason to disobey her. She is convinced that this man will make a mother out of me.

But a child will tear me apart. With one or five husbands—a mother is a mother, full of self sacrifice and pulled in all directions. Her desires buried deep under the path her child will walk.

Sem frowned, and I knew what he was thinking: a child would be his only guarantee. The only way to stop me from marrying another. I kissed him and stroked his cheek. But already I felt the gentle pulse of courtship throbbing inside my body.

So I cannot have this child they want so much. But now, I cannot be seen to actively prevent it. Sometimes in my dreams I hear this child calling me. Taking me somewhere I do not want to go. *Mother,* she says, *mother you belong to me.* I push her back and tell her it is not her time. That I am not a mother. I do not know if she will listen to me.

I hope the new husband will find his place. This time I am prepared for the changes ahead. Initially Shai will subside under the bright hue of new love. He will dance on the periphery, and I will find reprieve. A chance to breathe, to find stillness. But then, after a time, the old will seep back. I will be his again for a time at least. Until next time. For now, I hope my body will not betray me.

They are playing cards. I watch them ponder on each move; distrust leaks from their eyes onto their fingers. I hear a gentle tap at my door. I pause. I see Sem reappear from the kitchen and take his place among them. I sigh and wish once again that I could give him more. I open the door. There is a glass of warm water at my feet and a tiny handkerchief beside it. I unwrap the pale green cloth, staring at the fleshy balls that rest on my palm, pickled in lemon and ginger. There is no mistaking the soft ovaries. Pig, I am sure. I inhale and take a bite, savouring the taste for the first time. I smile with relief, grateful. The voices in my head diminish. Shai is gone. I see the next wedding—dancing and singing. I see my empty womb, my flat stomach. Then I see the tears in Sem's eyes. When I look closer, behind the sadness, I see fear, and then love.

college degree in tourism and service

tiphanie yanique

Sunshine is on the house. Rum and cola,
two for one. My mouth is sweet water.
I am faithful. I am your favorite.
I don't spit in the food. I lick it good.
I will bring it to you on a platter
flecked with skin. Ice cubes in the water
encasing a strand of my curly hair.
I will play steel pan with my wrists if it's
your birthday. But my hips are not polite.
Platitudes come free with the diploma.
Set the stick on fire. Move out the way.
I demonstrate the bending. Backward.
Good morning, sir. Have a nice stay,
ma'am. Welcome to my beautiful island.

possession

stephanie victoire

listen to me, I hear its voice whisper. I am sat in the corner of a motel room in absolute darkness, save for the intermittent winks of car lights passing by the window. I thought some stillness would calm it, shrink it down somehow so I could think clearly for a moment. But it talks to me in the quiet. It wants me to leave this room and head back out there, where there are salacious delights—where there are chances to intoxicate, exhilarate, and fornicate, to hurt someone else.

I was going to hurt him—my beloved, Eliot. If I'd stayed, for sure, I would have hurt him. I weep now for the humiliation he must have felt when I didn't show by his side at the altar today. The heartache he must be feeling now, I'm sure, is as powerful as this rage in me is to strangle someone. I had trembled standing outside the venue this afternoon where his family, our friends, bridesmaids and groomsmen awaited us, with anxiety for what I was about to do, and from the violence that was boiling up in my blood. I took off in the direction that would be Eliot's safety. I skimmed the boundaries of town, stomping along the edges of the woods by the highway in my wedding dress. No cars had passed by for an hour and the sun was beginning to set. My teeth chattered as the day's warmth left me. I stopped, exhausted, and swollen with anger. I screamed hot breath up into a cold, empty sky. But the demon held on inside me still. It clings to me.

I am now choking on my tears, and the thick dust and mustiness of the old motel carpet. It hates it when I feel weak. It makes greater efforts to puppet me. It tells me to leave this room and finish off the work it needs me to do; it pushes at me from the inside. The rage suddenly jumps up in me like vomit rising up the throat—I fight to push it down, to push the demon right down into the pit of my belly.

It has been riding me for some weeks now, and I'm not sure it will ever leave me until it has what it wants. On the day it came for me, I'd been in a rather sombre mood. Eliot had been away with work and the house had been too big without his footsteps and his laughter. To distract myself, I cleaned the house from east to west, trailing the path of the sun, listening to the songs of Chuck Berry, Connie Francis, Ritchie Valens, and Little Richard all day long—songs my mother used to play. I dusted ornaments I'd never dusted before, wiped skirting boards, scrubbed all crevices, sorted papers, and collected photographs absconded from their rightful places—the silly hair, dated clothes, and big grins of my family all tugged a smile from me. I found myself stroking the cheek of my little sister, Amy, who'd never wear that yellow dress again. I gave a small laugh to the retro moustache of my goofy father, who left this world the same time as Amy. I guess it was because she would have been too frightened to go alone, even towards heaven.

I was dizzy from the memories and from the cloying smells of pine furniture polish and disinfectant. My heart was swollen and heavy with melancholic nostalgia. I took several breaks for coffee and cigarettes, which steadied my feelings a little, and then I continued tidying and fixing until the early October evening stole the light.

I ate a meagre dinner of leftover grilled chicken and some bread, too tired to put together something colourful. After that, I let go of my bones in a piping hot bath and closed my eyes until something caused my heart to lurch. I didn't know what it was; there was no one there, no strange noises—just the normal acoustics of nothingness in the bathroom. But there was a smell that snagged on the rising steam of my bath water, the smell of rosemary and overturned earth.

I got out of the tub, walking into my bedroom to get dressed, and I was arrested again by the same scent. I felt the demon behind me, only I didn't know then what it was. I knew that I couldn't move, and I had no voice to scream. And the way it approached me from behind and walked its spindly fingers along the base of my neck round to my mouth, brushing my earlobes to savour all of me, I was suddenly seven years old again and Uncle

Richard was coming to tell me his stories. These nights would usually result in him finding comfort, after a woeful confession of his desires, on my belly, where he would then lift my nightshirt and place a kiss. He always came to see me in the shadows, just like every other man in my life before Eliot, finding their pleasure in the darkness of the world and the dark places inside of me.

Easy it went in, as light and agile as a spider, as weightless as a tendril of smoke. But I felt my heart harden as it wrapped itself around my innards, blanketed over all the tenderness and heat, and introduced my body and mind to hate.

It won some days, the demon. Times when I looked at Eliot's face and wanted to bully him, treat him like shit until I could see his tears. I wanted to actually taste them, as if they'd be made of sweet, dark liquor. If I had let my hands fly free at him, they would have scratched his face raw. But instead, with balled fists and a tightened jaw, I would go for a drive out of town and find the scummiest hole in which to do my deeds. I had one man seeing himself at the gates of hell for a minute while I held my hands around his neck and I rode him on top. The devil told him to come on in, but I decided to let his soul live this life a little while longer. I couldn't go through with it, and I felt a pain inside of my gut like my intestines were getting clenched up in a vice. The demon was angry with me for holding back, but I think I taught the man his lesson anyway. He stared right into my eyes and he froze with fear, went soft right there inside me. He then sobbed, cried an ugly cry as I got my clothes on and left. The demon had picked him out at a bar. It knew well enough who would test the limits with me. Thought he could stare at my body as if he owned it. That lick of the lips, the slow steady gaze up and down me, lingering around the tops of my thighs. It knew he'd been to some dark places in his mind too.

And after I found a bathroom where I washed myself up, I drove home and pulled my feelings in good and tight. The demon seemed a little spent after its work so I could feel some more of myself. Eliot greeted me at the door, happy to have me home.

"How's your mother doing?" he asked, his tone subdued, his eyelids a little heavy. I could see his long hours at work were getting to him, but he had waited up for me, I knew he would.

"She seemed worse this evening, so I stayed a while longer. Sorry I'm so late."

He held me for a while and I breathed in from the crease of his neck, the smell of his sandalwood, oakmoss, and blackberry cologne. The fragrance stirred the demon and began to show me things in my mind's eye. Eliot's body would be perfect for torturing—a slice here, a burn there. It pushed words up from the back of my throat to the tip of my tongue, words that would hurt Eliot, words that would offend and demean. But with lips firmly shut, I pulled away from him to go to bed, hoping that I'd just fall straight into a dreamless sleep. I didn't.

On a particularly black night, I tried to exorcise it. After I'd taken yet another man to the brink of death, the demon was riled again. *Finish him,* it always commanded, and I always disobeyed. I was vomiting spots of blood in the bathroom of a gas station. It had been having a tantrum, punching at my lungs, kicking at my stomach. I drove to the nearest church and walked straight in, hoping it would flee from my body right there on the steps. I pushed through the heavy wooden door, relieved to find it open. The smell of frankincense and the glow of a hundred candles seemed like heaven itself. I cupped some holy water from the stoup and swallowed it. It was cold, and tasted like the many hands that had taken from it. The demon didn't recoil from my drink, but rather laughed. I walked farther in and nearly took a seat in the back pew, but then saw the priest step down from the altar and smile at me. I feared for him instantly. He would have been the perfect sacrifice. The demon suddenly wanted him more than any other. By reflex, I performed the sign of the cross on myself and left.

It has been some hours since I entered this motel, and I have not moved from this spot on the floor. My cheeks are taut from dried tears, a dull throb has commenced at my temples. Where would Eliot be, this minute? Is he alone? He must curse me. Curse me for all of it. I am damned anyway. I have tried to make a plan, but my thoughts only come back to this blackness.

> It talks to me in the quiet.
> It shows me things in my mind's eye.

I see a naked woman, in a dark wood under an obsidian sky. There is no moon, but there are men with lanterns. Her arms are up above her head, wrists roped to the branch of a tree. She tries to shrink into herself, legs crossed to keep her sex out of sight, but it is not off their minds. They spit at her shaking body and occasionally stroke it. She is bruised around her sunken eyes. It is she. My demon. The men are speaking to her but I do not hear their words; only hers come through to me now:

Do it for all of us. Do it for the woman of me and the little girl of you.

Do it because of Uncle Richard's wandering fingers, lips, and tongue. Do it because of the ones that stole all of me. Do it because of those that think they own you.

She takes a hold of my beating heart and squeezes it. The pain has me clutching at my chest. I scream at her to let go. I have had enough. I stumble to my feet. I need air; I need a drink. I head out to find a bar, wearing my wedding dress and my dried tears, where some gentleman will buy me one.

mother

yomi sode

Iyaniwura, Baba nidingi — Mother is gold. Father is a
mirror

I think of the teeth you have lost
during pregnancy. Your breasts

that have lowered since giving birth.
At night I hear you. Deep mews of
lonely. Your heart left beating
on the strewed road of Ibadan,

the day you packed. Leaving a man
not worth fighting for.

night terrors

yomi sode

Do you see how many invitations I decline,
butting shirt hangers onto each other?

Each 'how are you finding it?' reminds me
night terrors carry little weight.

In this darkness, the street lamp writes
on our sparse wall like an epiphany.

I rock our boy to sleep, feel my stomach fold
over my belt. The excess fat slowly engulfs

the buckle like my father's. Tonight,
like most nights, growing old scares me.

wọ́n ti dé

yomi sode

Oyá,[1] our dead gradually make their way,
    bodies still warm from the gutting.

As you arrive, give her your names,
    Damilola, Carl, Mohammad, Derek.

Oyá, remind them of a home that resides
    in the *èkó* [2] sand between their toes,

        show each of your stillborn
        wrapped around your waist,

---

[1]   *Wọ́n ti dé = they have arrived. Oyá is the Orisha of winds, lightning, and violent storms, as well as Death and rebirth. She also keeps the gates of the cemetery.*

[2]   *Lagos*

yomi sode

èyin omo ololorun,[3] when walking to your graves,
hold her hand in calming your pierced hearts.

Oyá, are they scared as your gates open?
I would suggest you train some to be warriors,

though I doubt they knew
what they fought for whilst on earth.

Oyá,
Yansán[4]

Oyá-Iyansan[5]
guard them, as you would your own.

---

[3]   *You, children of God*
[4]   *also known as Oyá,*
[5]   *also known as Mother of nine*

129

roots

divya ghelani

"Quit your job!" you told me. You ran into the kitchen, flinging your leather jacket onto a chair. "We're going on a road trip!"

You kissed me, a hungry kiss filled with future. Then you held my hands and said you wanted adventure.

"I've seen too many movies and read too many books to be stuck in a shithole like this!" you said. "I want to live, to *see.*"

You poured yourself a cup of coffee and sloshed it about as you painted our future. I watched, mesmerised, as you spoke of volcanoes and pilgrimages, of towns without technology, of sunsets and sunrises, of ancient burial sites and jungles with snakes and orangutans. You looked so beautiful. Your face glowed with dreams of the future as you spoke of coral reefs and waterfalls, an underwater paradise. We made love on the kitchen floor, quickly and breathlessly, grasping at one another as if it were our last time. Satisfied, we wrapped ourselves in a blanket and fell asleep on the living room settee.

When I awoke it was early morning and the birds outside were going crazy. You were on your hands and knees, rummaging through your rucksack.

"Here," you said. "Take a look at these!"

You handed me a stack of tourist maps, flight details, printouts of traveller blogs. You'd even bought a box of malaria tablets from Boots. All we had to do was save up, buy the tickets, book the accommodation. You had the whole thing planned out.

"You *want* to come, don't you?" you said.

Your hand was on my hip, just how I liked it. I stood in silence as you moved in close to tell me you loved me. Your lips sealed the deal. You were always running ahead of me, a skyscraper on legs, and I was always struggling to keep up. Deep down I thought, "If I stop I will die." Your dazzling curls, your confidence, your arguments that shone, your knowing grin. Could you hear me running behind you, breathless, my bones aching? How long do you think that could have lasted, Adam? How long?

You won me over. Of course you did. My fear of leaving home was not as great as my fear of losing you. For months we ate cheap meals and did overtime in our bullshit jobs, whispering travel plans to bored coworkers. We forfeited our yearly cinema passes in favour of illegally streamed movies. We cut each other's hair. We stopped buying organic, committed to flasks instead of coffee shops. We used the public library instead of Am-

131

azon. I made my own wax from sugar and lemon, tearing up old bed sheets for the strips just like my mother had taught me.

You wanted to see everything and I wanted pull you in, my dragon kite in the high winds. The size of your dreams awed and scared me so I suggested the US for the first leg of our trip.

"You never know," I said. "We might run out of money sooner than we think. And I'd like to see the US, just once in my life. It's not exotic but it sort of is, too, what with all that culture, all those movies we've seen."

You acquiesced and I sighed with relief. We made love and talked into the night. It was like we were growing our very own magical baby.

One day in late spring when the leaves were beginning to fall, it happened. You logged on to our joint bank account after payday and discovered that we'd met our target by saving eight thousand pounds. Eight thousand pounds! You were too excited to sleep and spent the whole night sitting in bed with your laptop Googling the places we'd visit after the US: Thailand and Nepal, Jamaica, Peru. My mind drifted from one strange dream to another. In the morning, you told me we should hand in our notices at the same time and then message each other when it was done. We threw an impromptu party at home that evening. Everyone got drunk and silly and you climbed onto the kitchen table and toasted me. You said you were "crazy" about your Sita and that I was the sexiest, most brilliant woman you'd ever met. We were going to "shag our way across the world!" Our friends roared their approval.

Both sets of parents arrived to see us off at the railway station. Yours kissed us goodbye, two pecks on each cheek. Mine hugged me and cried and told us to be in contact every day. My mother, in her blue and gold sari and black cardigan, was tense and anxious. She had prepared a *puro* in tissue paper, tied together with red string. She pressed it into my palms for good luck, her eyes darting between you and me. My father called after you as we headed over to the platform.

"Adam!" he said. "When you come home, marry Sita. Settle down. Get jobs. Have children. I'm an old man. I am not from your generation. But I know life."

I recall the knot in my mother's eyebrows as my father spoke, the strange way my suitcase felt both heavy and light.

We laughed and joked through that train journey. On the long flight to Los Angeles airport, we held each others' hands, dozed and snogged, watched movies and comedy shows. We laughed and pulled faces, peeling the tinfoil from our dinky in-flight meals. Sometimes I placed my head on your shoulder. Sometimes I awoke and watched you doze.

In Los Angeles, we took a cab from the airport to El Segundo. There we ate In and Out burgers just like the man in the travelogue had recommended. Then we headed to a car rental place where the Indian man at the desk spoke to me in Hindi until he saw that I was with you. You looked through his catalogue of cars and chose a cheap little Ford, all black and shiny, with a CD player for your music and a big drinks holder on the driver's side.

"My girlfriend can't even read a map," you told him.

He shrugged his shoulders and smiled.

In LA the roads were long and wide and for three weeks, we drove along the West Coast. It was like starring in our very own movie, a biopic of our lives. I stretched my feet on the dashboard to paint my toenails blue, watched as they sparkled and dried in the setting sun. Your music collection became the soundtrack to our journey: Prince, Sly and the Family Stone, Stevie Wonder, Al Green…and the sea was pretty and crackly, unreal and sparkling, as if some giant hand had reached out of the sky and covered it in cellophane.

We walked along beaches at sunset, gathering seashells, the cool sea air reminding me of salt and vinegar chips. We marvelled at rich people's beach houses, their once-beautiful exteriors bashed and roughed up by the ocean, a great leveller. We found our own beaches too. They were private by default because when we turned up early morning or late at night there wasn't another soul in sight. The lights that twinkled along the bay seemed so distant.

We visited beaches with malls and shops. We roamed and loitered, ate lollypops, stripped to our bikinis and shorts, paddled in the sea, kissed and held hands, sunsets and sunrises, sand in your shoes, sunglasses on, sunglasses off, dry martinis and sex, 'bust-your-stomach-open-and-go-to-sleep' spaghetti meatballs, the massive sun turned into tiny bits of glitter in the sand. Adam, do you remember those sea lions lying on that beach like fat moustachioed sunbathers? Do you remember those seagulls perched on the top of our car, fighting for food? Saccharine memories, like that pecan pie we ate in Sally's Café with its cheerful rainbow sign. More sunrises and sunsets, more golden beaches, more pecan pies, more bottomless cups of cheap bullshit coffee. And do you remember that bitch you couldn't take your eyes off, the one who looked like the seventeen-year-old temp at your work? I turned my gaze to the water. There, a majestic-looking white boat with big white sails was heading towards the horizon, as if to fall off the edge of the earth.

At night, we stayed in Motel 6s that felt too anonymous to make love in. Sometimes they stank of smoke even though we'd specifically booked the nonsmoking rooms. Sometimes the faceless neighbours made weird noises. Their weirdness bought us closer and we held hands in the dark, discussing our dreams for the future. You kept talking about how you were "woke" to your purpose in life, how you never wanted to go home. "What was home anyway?" you said. You wanted to see as much as the world had to offer, to taste, to feel. I thought of our parents, yours and mine, the little town market we had left behind, the allotment patch. Suddenly, I sat up.

"What about children?" I said. "And marriage?"

You shrugged your shoulders.

"What about it?" you said, your eyes mocking. "Do you really believe in all that crap?"

Did I? Were those even my dreams? Hadn't my mother suffered? I listened and nodded, feeling confused and strange.

Forget it, I told myself. *Life is now. Moment by moment, and Adam loves you. This trip is time you'll never get back.* As the road unfolded before us my other dreams felt strange and foolish. They were so pedestrian beside yours, monstrous in their littleness. And how could I blame you with your heart so full of the world? I empathised. I recalled that big suburban house in your childhood, the cold two-pecks-on-the-cheek parents you were both running from and towards.

You drove our little black Ford towards Yosemite National Park in the central Sierra Nevada of California. By the time we reached it, the weather had changed so much that it felt as if a film set had imported in foreign goblets of snow. Big fat snowflakes seemed to spit out of the cold sky, coating the tall regal pines that lined the road we were traveling on. Everything felt so strange and unseasonal, like Christmas in summer.

The park guide, in her earmuffs and scarf, sent us back to the store on the road to buy tyre tracks. She said there had been accidents in the past and that Yosemite was dangerous in the snow. The tyre tracks were so expensive they made you worry about our money reserves for the whole trip. We stood at the store, eating sandwiches and procrastinating. But by the time we chose some tracks, a whole hour had passed and the snow had stopped completely. The shopkeeper laughed and told us we were off the hook. He said it was destiny.

divya ghelani

The views inside Yosemite National Park were awesome, nothing like I had ever imagined. Our jaws dropped in wonder that the United States could look like this. Even you, with your guidebooks and maps, seemed surprised.

We drove in silence and I photographed the whole place with my eyes, a series of postcards to send home: evergreens in snow, crazy-coloured skies, mist on the mountains, streams gurgling through cracked rocks. It opened you up just knowing a place like that existed. It made you breathe deeper.

When the sky began to darken, we drove back to the main entrance gates. It was off-peak season, so we rented one of the more expensive cottages just outside. It looked so wooden and rustic but inside was America: big TVs and electric tin openers, a pink-cushioned bed and homemade cookies next to a "Welcome Honeymooners!" card. We had sex. I held you back as I guided you in, negotiating the distance between us.

Early next morning, while you slept, I opened the shutters to see the iconic view advertised in the cottage brochure. All I could see was a sea of thick and oppressive fog. It was as if there had been a silent war that night, foreign bombings we hadn't been aware of. Or else it was as if a massive forest fire had ripped through everything, leaving only the honeymoon suite on the hill. I closed the shutters, feeling the mist in my bones. Awake, you looked out onto an altogether different sky: the fog had turned to thin mist and we drank coffee, watching the hazy white tips of mountaintops, snowy

like the Himalayas. We took up our rucksacks and headed towards the big trees.

"On the website it says they're so big," you enthused,
"you'll think you're dreaming."

You said it was always a secret destination of yours, to
come to the US and see sequoias. When you were a little
boy, your grandfather had showed you the pictures of
them in *Reader's Digest*. You'd finished a whole string of
wildlife books, but the one with the big trees had kept
you dreaming. You'd clean forgotten about the book
and yet here we were heading to see the sequoias.

"Think of it, Sita!" you said. "A tree so big and wide
that if you cut a hole into its trunk, you could take a
truck and drive right through!"

"No," I said. "It can't be true."

But Yosemite has many wonders. Tioga Road, Tu-
olumne Meadows, Hetchy Hetchy, and Crane Flat all
distracted us with their wondrous displays. We saw the
falls and the beautiful valley from Glacier Point, after which we headed back to our honeymoon cottage.
When we finally reached the Mariposa Grove of Giant
Sequoias, it was day three of our park visit and the sun
was setting, bleeding its peaches and light blues into the
sky. We parked our little black Ford in the designated car
park and stepped out to find the giant trees. The red-
woods had been so enormous, I had thought of *Jack and
the Bean Stalk*. But, Adam, the sequoia trees were straight
out of a more wondrous tale entirely. So storyish, they
were the origin of stories. It was their realness that made

138

them magical. I pressed my palms against the bark of a younger one. It felt rough and smooth.

"Whoa!" you said, clicking pictures with your mobile phone. "Amazing!"

I left you to it, wandering beyond the designated path, venturing farther into the forest. After a few minutes of walking alone, the tourists seemed to fall away. Silence breathed. You were both near and far. I gazed up at the one or two stars that were making themselves known and then all of a sudden I was wandering in mist. Moments later, I found myself confronted with largest tree I'd ever seen. Mist covered its branches.

"Cold, isn't it?" said a voice.

"What?" I said, looking about.

"No," it said. "I'm here."

I looked about me but again, no one. I did a full circle of the sequoia's massive trunk, passing its wooden sign, which read "The Grizzly Giant." I looked up, too, as high as I could, but the tree's enormous branches and leaves seemed to be made of mist. I gazed at the tree's trunk. It featured a blackened hole and I remembered a park guide telling us of a big forest fire long ago. He said some of the animals had died of fright long after the fire ravaged their home: post-traumatic stress syndrome. I stepped over the fence that guarded the tree from visitors. My fingers searched the blackened hole. It was soft and tender, as if someone had burnt the tree's heart out. As I examined my black-stained fingers, I asked myself, *Was it ... speaking to me? Could it be true?*

"You know," said the tree, "this whole place used to look so different. *I* used to look so different. Once upon

139

a time, so long ago. Your name, Sita. It means 'daughter of the earth.'"

My heart began to race. How could it know?

"Don't worry," it said. "I know…it's not normal. And yet, here we were. You and I."

"What happened?" I asked. "What's happening?"

"Life," replied the tree. "Changes."

"How are you speaking to me? From where?"

"We're speaking one soul to another. I know you don't believe it, but you feel it, don't you? When I saw you, I said to myself, 'That is a woman looking for roots, a place to pitch up and call home.' How could I know?" said the tree, reading my thoughts. "I see you, Sita. You were born into this world and you were loved. Now… you're wounded. There's been a fire…you're burnt out inside. Believe me, I know. Here, in this other place, you don't know who you are. Look at the sky above you."

The mist began to clear, and I saw the tree in its immensity.

"See those branches that reach upwards and out? They exist because I am rooted. I know what you are. I know what you need."

My voice had left me, and it felt as if the entire forest was hallucinating. I saw my mother in a sari made of the tree's leaves, her nervous hands on the *puro*, the gold bangles that would be mine when I married him.

"You mustn't think of it as a betrayal. Being truly selfish is the greatest gift you can give. What are you to yourself when you feel like a ghost, like the mist and the fog?"

Adam was nowhere to be seen. The tourists too were long gone. The sky above was starry, a million silver eyes watching.

"What doesn't make you happy won't make him happy."

"I don't know what you're talking about," I stammered. "I...he's my..."

"I came here long ago, Sita, with a burnt-out heart. I was searching for answers, but I needed to learn that which I had forgotten. I've seen such things...horror and beauty, sights to turn your dry, blackened heart sweet once more."

"How have you?" I asked, suddenly defiant. "You live in one place all these years. That sign says you're thirty-three hundred years old. You're stuck in the mud."

"You need to know how to look, Sita. You need to pay attention. That's why you're here. Or have you forgotten? Let me teach you."

"I don't know what you're talking about..." I said, backing away.

There was a man, I told myself. A strange man behind the tree and he was going to come out and murder me. Adam would remember me. He'd come get me. He loved—

Just then the ground beneath me began to tremble and shake.

"Come home," the tree said.

"I think...we're going to get married," I told the tree. "Marry me."

"No. He's...I don't know..."

141

"Still…after all this time you don't know? Here is home. A real home…you'll see."

The ground beneath my feet began to rumble. The earth cracked and split and soon enough the roots of the sequoia tree were upturning huge chunks of soil. Their ropes looked so beautiful. They rose up like magical ten-drils, moved like dancing snakes, enticing me, pulling me towards them. They stroked my skin, my long black hair. They felt so … sweet.

"And if I say no," I said, my voice trembling as I pushed them away.

"How can you say no to home?"

"What's it like in there?" I asked as the trees roots lift-ed me like a tiny doll in their hands. I touched the bark of the tree. It felt both rough and soft.

"You are god. You are everything."

What happened next was something I could never have foreseen, not in my wildest dreams. You see, my heart opened. My beating heart burst in the cage of my chest and spilled out of my flesh like a cracked egg. It oozed from me, Adam, and that's how the tree took it.

They say sequoias are old souls, and I know what they mean. Living in here, within this giant of life, I know more than I've ever known. I see *feelingly*. The movement of a bird's wing is a miracle, and when even one droplet of rain falls on one of my leaves, an ecstasy of small vi-brations rushes through me. The nearest stream, though far, far away, reaches me like echoes in a human dream. I sense fear in animals, feel the life pulsing blood through their legs when they are chased. My branches reach up to other worlds, and my many hands are shade for animals and humans and insects and plants like me. I am a resting place between flights, and the birds who dream in clouds above me procreate and make their homes in me. Tenacity and intelligence is my nature. I reach for the sun and give to others as they give it to me. I see changes all the time. Here, we give birth to one another. In the springtime squirrels scurry about me, delighting me with their tickling. And in the winter, the frost settles on my bones. I sleep with my inner eye open.

Every millisecond, Adam, is clear to me, and every moment in this earth is a blessing, a series of blessings, transformation. I have seen the growth and decay of my fellow trees. It is nothing and everything. I saw you, too. I don't remember how long we were together or how long we have been apart. But I recall how you searched for me with police officers, the cars and the torches, the dogs on leashes. You called my parents from your mobile phone. I watched, interested, in a distant sort of way. And then years later, we met again. You returned to the scene of my "disappearance" with a dazzling new woman. Her name was Patience Yin and she'd borne you two children. They were beauties, Adam. I loved their vigour and excitement. They climbed over the fence that surrounds me and touched my bark. Their squeals and pleasure rippled through me and I felt glad for you, for the new life you'd created. You encircled me with your sorrow before retreating for ice cream. Adam, when you left with Patience's children that were somehow also mine, you became nothing more than ghosts to me. A series of recurring echoes and memories. I

143

let you go and watched peacefully as thoughts of you passed me by.

Time loops around me like the concentric circles in my trunk. Beyond the peace and rest of the forest and the soil, a tiredness has set in, a feeling of restlessness. I hold it inside me for so long until one day, he comes. I feel the stranger before I see him, and when I see him I know him. Somehow I know what to do, too. He is tall and slim with curly black hair. He smells fragrant, unusual somehow. There is a green tattoo on his hand, the shape of a leaf.

"Cold, isn't it?" I say.

"Who's there? Who's speaking to me?" he says, his eyes filled with wonder.

"I'm in here," I tell him. "And you look like a man in search of roots, a place to call home…"

samo as everybody else

irfan master

dearest mister sir basquiat

/| i like to write ~~jazz~~ poetry dont like to use full stops or commas or grammar stuff because thats not how I think and i like to cross things out like you do ~~just be=cause~~ and sometimes because its not at the top of my head >> is that the same with you? i like question marks and they do have a full stop but that's different isnt it?

>> i like symbols too because they seem mysterious and maybe the beginnings of another language you see? //||^^+≠

^ i live in care which is weird because i dont feel like i live in care if you know what i mean?

^ i should ask you a proper question probably the ones

ive crossed out can still be good questions just a bit hidden

^ive got to go but will write more ive got things i want to say/~~ask~~

>> j-ka

irfan master

nearest mister sir basquiat

æ am 15 from queens >> and the world dont make ~~no sense~~ except your drawings and paintings and writings which make ~~no sense~~ also but to me

im writing you so you think im smart and have something to say because the people ≥≥here≤≤ ~~they~~ think ive nothing to say and that symbols dont mean nothing and crossing things out dont mean nothing and circling things dont mean nothing and writing onto paintings dont mean nothing and drawing only in the corner of the page dont mean nothing i mean nothing means nothing so what >>?

≠≠ the last thing my pops got me before he ~~had to go~~ was a set of ++colour pencils long and shiny with silver letters and thick lead

++ the last thing my moms got me before she ~~had to go~~ were a pair of dungarees with patches on them she sprayed graffiti on the back to make me happy

≥≥ never used the too nice pencils swapped them one time for money

^^ does that make me less like you? does that make you like me less?

//write back >> ~~even if its crossed out~~
>j-ka

147

fairest mister sir Basquiat

list to be scooby doo done

$\geq$ steal some paints
$\leq$ ask you some ~~uncrossed out questions~~
$\leq$ say no to taking the pretty pink pills
$\geq$ say no to taking the bitter blue pills
$\geq$ say no to the care manager

ive seen your word lists they dont make no sense but at least they are in the right order ~~[978645221]~~ ~~[lnmopsqst-vu]~~
~~writing is harder than not writing and youre making me write a lot~~

>j-ka

psssst wish you were ~~w>here~~ they said you were

irfan master

fairest dearest mister sir Basquiat

im sorry I havent written as ive not been myself recently
which is stupid as thats who ive always wanted to be

i was sad too as ~~they~~ shaved my head

id been growing it out so it looked a bit like yours angles
sharp ends but it made me look a bit much ~~they~~ said and
it was easier/~~better~~ to take it off ~~they~~ said

im a bit ~~much two much~~ even for mine self
but i miss playing with mine hair ≫≫≫≫≫

i ~~know~~ youre samo
i ~~know~~ im not samo
i ~~know~~ youre not samo
i ~~know~~ im/youre samo

>j-ka

nearest dearest michel basquiat

i got arrested once for chalking street magic
i got arrested once for asking the way home
~~i once arrested myself before i got myself arrested~~
i got choked out once for saying i was ~~anti~~ samo
i got choked out once for saying i was ~~anti~~ dreaming
~~i got choked out once for saying i was anti psychotic~~
^^^^ ^^^^^   ^^^^

>j-ka

irfan master

sir samo michel basquiat

once upon a time there was a black king...

once upon a time there was a black king
~~once upon a time there was a black king~~
~~once upon a time there was a black king~~
~~once upon a time there was a black king~~
~~once upon a time there was a black king~~
~~once upon a time there was a black king~~
~~once upon a time there was a black king~~
~~once upon a time there was a black king~~
~~once upon a time there was a black king~~
~~once upon a time there was a black king~~
~~once upon a time there was a black king~~

the end
~~rides off into sunset~~
~~gets the girl~~
~~saves the human race~~
~~wins the shootout at the uh oh corral~~

>j-ka

151

young king basquiat

ok ok i got a ~~question~~ / |
>>>>>>>>>>> i look a bit like you / | you look bits
like ~~me~~ what happens to the next one who looks like ~~us~~?

ask samo >>> he might know?

irfan master

mister michel basquiat

its harder to write you good now <-> they say im wasting
away god given grace and flavour but ~~they~~ dont choke
me no more not here but now ~~they~~ say im ant! psychotic
and the pink+blue pills make me dream violent dreams
>>>

dont wanna dream ~~they~~ dreams no more dont wanna be
ant! no more dont wanna be samo no more dont wanna
be almost famous no more dont wanna say shit to fit no
more dont wanna say nuthin didnt do nuthin no more
dont wanna say ima jazz poet no more dont wanna hear
hands up no more dont wanna hear my rights no more
dont wanna hear pops alto sax no more dont wanna see
queens no more dont wanna see mine self in mirrors
no more dont wanna see dont wanna see /////// dont
wanna see anyone no more /////////////// no
more ///////// no more ///////// no more
////////   /////////////

>j-ka

Dear Mr Basquiat,

I am writing as a representative of child protection services in New York to apologise on behalf of the board of which I am Director. It has come to our attention that a young charge of ours has been writing you notes, letters etc. It is a strict policy of ours to not allow our charges to write to people they do not know or are strangers to them. This young boy, who I am unable to name for confidential reasons, came to us a few months ago now after being arrested as a vagrant more times than was reasonable. Fortunately, we were able to offer a diagnosis and he has, since being with us, improved and is now onto the next stage of his treatment. It was unknown to us that he was, on what is a weekly group walk downtown, posting these notes into a gallery that represents you and your work. It has only come to our attention because your letter was opened by an orderly at the facility and forwarded to me. Now, I understand the sentiment you are trying to portray to the boy, but your intervention in this situation will not help him. The next phase of his treatment will dramatically improve his behaviour and instil in him a sense of character and identity. His marked improvement on a series of anti-psychotic drugs has made him a more introspective member of the facility, and I want to assure you that he will be well looked after, but we must give him the time for the treatment to fully assert itself before the changes are felt deep within his mind. I fully understand why you felt you needed to write to him, but will ask now that you refrain from any further contact with him. He is at the best possible place for him, you can be sure of that.

On a side note, I myself am a huge art lover. Mainly the old masters of the renaissance period, Michelangelo, Titian, Caravaggio. Great works that spread the love of ideas, philosophy, and offer a social commentary of the times. Artists still relevant today here in New York. I have only seen your work in magazines Mr Basquiat, and although no expert, I can't say I'm drawn to the free form style you portray, the lurid and messy canvases you offer and this incessant crossing out of text that is then indecipherable is beyond my understanding of what art is. I'm not saying your work isn't art, I'm not an art critic, but if I were to offer anything, it would be this. Surely art must show us something about ourselves when we look at it and be a commentary for its time? Surely it must have a level of technical ability that must be considered a minimum before one is offered a place at the table? Surely it must ring through the ages and still be relevant decades, centuries later?

These are just the thoughts of a humble man with a passion for art. Just my two cents.

Again, please accept my apologies on behalf of the board, and I wish you all the best with your future artistic endeavours.

Yours sincerely,
A. K. Brandt
Director of Child Protection Services
The State of New York

bare lit anthology

M̲

nearest dearest fairest > j-ka

i have no answers to questions
but samo does and samo says

~~never give up~~
~~never give up~~
~~never give up~~
~~never give up~~
~~never give up~~
~~never give up~~
~~never give up~~
~~never give up~~
~~never give up~~
~~never give up~~
~~never give up~~
~~never give up~~
~~never give up~~
~~never give up~~
~~never give up~~

JEAN-MICHEL BASQUIAT

about the editors

Kavita Bhanot is a writer, editor, teacher, activist based between India and England. Her fiction, nonfiction, and reviews have been published widely in anthologies, magazines, journals, newspapers, and online forums, including Media Diversified, Round Table India, and The Independent. Her short stories have been broadcast on BBC Radio 4. She is editor of the anthology *Too Asian, Not Asian Enough* (Tindal Street Press, 2011) and the forthcoming *Book of Birmingham* (Comma Press, 2017). She has a PhD from Manchester University in Creative Writing and Literature, has taught at Manchester University and Fordham University, and is a reader and mentor with the Literary Consultancy.

Courttia Newland is the author of seven works of fiction including his debut, *The Scholar*. His latest novel, *The Gospel According to Cane*, was published in 2013 and has been optioned by Cowboy Films. He was nominated for the Impac Dublin Literary Award, the Frank O'Connor Award, the CWA Dagger in the Library Award, the Hurston/Wright Legacy Award, and the Theatre 503 Award for playwriting, as well as numerous others. His short stories have appeared in many anthologies and been broadcast on BBC Radio 4. In 2016, he was awarded the Taner Baybars Award for science fiction writing and the Roland Rees Bursary for playwriting. He is associate lecturer in creative writing at the University of Westminster and is completing a PhD in creative writing.

Mend Mariwany is a writer, editor, and cultural curator with an MA in Postcolonial Theory from Goldsmiths, University of London. He was born in Iraq and was raised in Germany before moving to the UK, where he cofounded Bare Lit Festival in 2016. Mend has organised arts events and storytelling performances and worked with a range of magazines, including *Muftah, Media Diversified,* and *Skin Deep.* He is currently based in London, where he is working on his debut collection of poetry and prose.

about the authors

Raymond Antrobus is a British-Jamaican poet, performer, and educator, born and bred in Hackney. He is one of the world's first recipients of an MA in Spoken Word education from Goldsmiths University. His poems have been published in *Poetry* magazine (US), *Poetry Review*, *The Rialto*, *Magma Poetry*, *The Deaf Poet's Society*, and forthcoming in *Wasafiri*, University of Arkansas Press, and Bloodaxe, *Ten Anthology*. His first pamphlet, *Shapes & Disfigurements of Raymond Antrobus* (2012), is published by Burning Eye Books. His second pamphlet, *To Sweeten Bitter* (2017), is published by Out-Spoken Press. His debut poetry collection will be published by Penned in the Margins (2018).

Sharmila Chauhan is a screenwriter, playwright, and prose writer: fascinated by the quiet meanings of peoples' lives, her work is often a transgressive meditation on love, sex, and an exploration of the diasporic experience. She has written three short films and one feature. Most recently, her short film *Oysters* was commissioned by Film London (2016). She was also part of the Film London–Cinestan Microschool (2016), where she developed her feature *Heart of the City*. Her plays include *The Husbands* (an exploration of polyandry and matriarchy in India, Soho Theatre), *Born Again / Purnajanam* (Southwark Theatre), and well as *10 Women* (with Bethan Dear, Avignon Festival). Shortlisted for the Asian New Writer Award (2009 and 2012), Sharmila's short stories have been published widely in print and online. She is currently working on her novel *Seven Mirrors* and is Artist in Residence at the Tagore Centre London and a curator for the South Asian Women's Creative Collective (SAW-CC), London. Sharmila also has a degree in pharmacy and a PhD in clinical pharmacology from University College London. She lives in London with her husband, children, and cat, Tashi. www.sharmilathewriter.com

Vera Chok is an actor, writer, and performance maker particularly interested in investigating sex, shame, race, loss, connection, and comedy. On the page or live, she manipulates language and space to create experiential pieces. Her piece "Yellow" is a chapter in *The Good Immigrant*, a bestselling collection of essays exploring what it means to be an ethnic minority in Britain today. Her writing has been featured by *Rising, Brautigan Free Press,* and *Yauatcha Life,* and performed at the inaugural Bare Lit Festival. www.verachok.org

Selma Dabbagh is a British Palestinian writer of fiction who lives in London. Her writing is mainly set in the contemporary Middle East, though it doesn't have to be. Recurring themes to date are idealism (however futile), placelessness, political engagement (or lack thereof), and the impact of social conformity on individuals. Selma's first novel, *Out of It*, was published by Bloomsbury in 2011 and 2012 (pbk) and was nominated as a Guardian Book of the Year in 2011 and 2012. The Arabic edition, *Gaze Tahta Al-Jild* (Gaza under the Skin), translated by Khulood Amr, was published by BQFP in August 2015. Selma has written and published numerous short stories with *Granta*, *Wasafiri*, International PEN, and others. She wrote an Imison Award–nominated radio play produced by BBC Radio 4, *The Brick* (broadcast in January 2014). She has also produced numerous blogs and pieces of journalism for newspapers and magazines from *The Guardian* and the *LRB* in the UK to *GQ* in India.

Martin De Mello is a short fiction writer and poet based in Manchester. His poems and short stories have appeared in several anthologies, including Peepal Tree's *Red: Contemporary Black British Poetry*. He has a poetry collection, *if our love stays above the waist*, published by Flipped Eye.

Divya Ghelani holds an MA in Creative Writing from the University of East Anglia and an MPhil in Literary Studies from the University of Hong Kong. She is working on the completion of her debut novel, which was longlisted for the 2016 Deborah Rogers Writers' Award, the 2016 SI Leeds Literary Award, and received an honorary mention in the Harry Bowling Prize for New Writing. She was a 2016 apprentice at London's premier short story salon, The Word Factory, and has been writing lots of new short stories.

Poet and author of literary memoir *Springfield Road* (Unbound) and poetry books *Fishing in the Aftermath: Poems, 1994-2014* (Burning Eye) and *Under the Pier* (Nasty Little Press), **Salena Godden** was shortlisted for this year's Ted Hughes Award for new work in poetry with her spoken word album *LIVEwire*, released with independent spoken word label Nymphs and Thugs. She has been shortlisted for 'Best Spoken Word Performer' in the Saboteur Awards 2017. The short fiction published in this anthology, "Blue Cornflowers," was shortlisted for the 4th Estate and Guardian short story prize in 2016. Her essay "Shade" was published in *The Good Immigrant*, which was championed by J. K. Rowling and crowdfunded and published with Unbound. It featured as a Radio 4 book of the week and won the Readers Choice Book of the Year Award. Most recently, *The Good Immigrant* has been shortlisted in the nonfiction category of the British Book Awards. www.salenagodden.co.uk

Tendai Huchu's first novel, *The Hairdresser of Harare*, was released in 2010 to critical acclaim and has been translated into several languages. His multigenre short stories and nonfiction have appeared in the *Manchester Review, Interzone, Space and Time Magazine, Ellery Queen*

Mystery Magazine, *The Africa Report*, *Wasafiri*, and else-where. Between projects, he translates fiction between the Shona and English languages. His new novel is *The Maestro, the Magistrate and the Mathematician*. Find him @ TendaiHuchu or on www.tendaihuchu.com.

Jennifer Nansubuga Makumbi is a Ugandan novelist and short story writer based in Manchester. She has a PhD from Lancaster University. Jennifer has taught Creative Writing and English for the last ten years in British Universities. Her novel, *Kintu*, won the Kwani Manuscript Project in 2013. It was published in 2014 and was longlisted for the Etisalat Prize 2014. Jennifer has published numerous short stories. Her short story "Lets Tell This Story Properly" won the overall Commonwealth Short Story Prize 2014. In 2015 she won an Arts Council Grant to research her second novel, *The First Woman Was Fish*. Her short story "Malik's Door" came out in *Closure: A Black British Anthology* in October 2015. Jennifer is currently working on a collection of short stories set in Manchester, which will form her third book.

Irfan Master is the author of *A Beautiful Lie*, which was published by Bloomsbury in 2011 and was shortlisted for the Waterstone's Children's Book Prize and Branford Boase Award for debut authors. It also featured on the 2013 USSBY Outstanding International Book Honour List. A story about Partition for a graphic novel anthology, *This Side, That Side*, was published by Yoda Press in 2013. In the same year, he had a short story adapted by Booktrust into a touring show aimed at Bangladeshi, Pakistani, and Somali families; the tour visited prisons, libraries, and community centres to encourage and celebrate storytelling. In 2014, Irfan was commissioned to write a radio play by Leicester University as part of their hidden stories project. He was also published in an anthology of Leicester writers in 2016 by Dahlia Publishing with a short story that was nominated by the publisher for the Pushcart Prize. His forthcoming novel for young adults, *Out of Heart*, will be published by Hot Key Books in 2017.

Selina Nwulu is a writer and a poet. Her first chapbook collection, *The Secrets I Let Slip*, was published by Burning Eye Books in September 2015 and is a Poetry Book Society recommendation. Selina has toured with her poetry both nationally and internationally, as well having performed at Glastonbury, Edinburgh Fringe, and StAnza Poetry Festival, St Andrews, where she was reviewed as "an emerging writer to watch," and Cúirt Literature Festival in Galway. She has been commissioned by Apples and Snakes, the RSA, A New Direction and the Free Word Centre and was Young Poet Laureate for London 2015–16, a prestigious award that recognizes talent and potential in the capital.

Kajal Odedra is a British Indian writer and activist from the Midlands. She writes fiction and poetry about identity, religion, and politics. She is currently working on her first novel about an Indian immigrant family living in nineties Britain during the rise of New Labour. Her activism has included campaigning on reforming politics, women's rights, and racial justice issues. She has written opinion pieces for *The Guardian* and *Huffington Post* and advises about gender and racial diversity in the tech industry. Kajal's roots are in India and Uganda, where her parents immigrated from in the 1970s. She is currently living in Hackney, London, and pursuing a Master's in Creative Writing at Goldsmiths, University of London.

Hibaq Osman is a Somali writer born and based in West London. Her work centres largely around women, identity, and the healing process. She is a current member of both the Burn After Reading and Octavia collectives, with the aim to help foster writing communities that showcase talent, drive, and understanding. No stranger to the stage, Hibaq has participated in various slams, festivals, and poetry nights across the UK since 2012. Often taken from real life experiences, Hibaq's writing focuses on the hidden aspects of our lives and how we can bring the unspoken to the forefront. As a member of Octavia—a group of women of colour poets—she works towards a future where funding and access to the arts for people of colour is considered the norm and not an exception. Outside of the poetry world, Hibaq is a recent Psychology and Counselling graduate with a desire to expand mental health service access to people who fall on various intersections of identity. In the future she aims to use poetry and prose writing as a way to help others examine trauma, come to terms with the past, and work on positively moving towards a healthier understanding of self. In her free time she runs dance classes, is failing at learning two languages, and tweets too much.

Koye Oyedeji's writing has appeared in a number of publications, including *Virginia Quarterly Review*, *Wasafiri Magazine*, and the *Washington City Paper* Fiction Issue. He has contributed to collections such as *The Fire People* (Canongate Press), *IC3: The Penguin Book of Black British Writing* (Penguin), and, more recently, the anthology *Closure* (Peepal Tree). The short story "Postscript from the Black Atlantic" was shortlisted for the Wasafiri 2015 New Writers Prize. He was recently shortlisted for a Miles Moreland Writing Scholarship and is currently at work on a collection of short stories and a novel.

Yomi Sode balances the fine line between Nigerian and British cultures, which can be humorous, loving, self-reflective, and, at times, uncomfortable. Over the past nine years, Yomi has had work commissioned by The Mayor's Office, BBC World Service/BBC Africa, Channel 4, various charities, and recently presented a poem at the UN Humanitarian Summit. In 2014, he won a place on Nimble Fish's *RE: Play* programme to develop his one-man show *COAT*. The scratch of *COAT* has since been programmed in festivals held by Southbank and Roundhouse to sold-out audiences. In September 2016, Yomi traveled to New York as part of the British Council's Shakespeare Lives initiative to read his work at the New York Public Library. As part of this initiative, he also facilitated workshops in schools as well as reading in various poetry organisations. In 2017, a selection of Yomi's poems will be published alongside nine other poets in *The Complete Works* anthology, a national development programme for advanced Black and Asian writers in the UK.

Stephanie Victoire was born in London to a French-Creole Mauritian family. In 2010 she graduated with a BA in Creative Writing from London Metropolitan University. In 2014 Stephanie completed her collection of fairy and folk tales entitled *The Other World, It Whispers* whilst on the Almasi League writers' programme. Two of these stories were separately published in 2015 and the collection itself is published with Salt, November 2016; the book was longlisted for the Saboteur Awards and the Edge Hill Prize. Stephanie will have a short story aired on BBC Radio 4 in September 2017. She is currently working on a novel, *The Heart Note*. www.stephanievictoire.com

Tiphanie Yanique is the author of the poetry collection *Wife*, which won the 2016 Bocas Prize in Caribbean poetry and the United Kingdom's 2016 Forward / Felix Dennis Prize for a first collection. She is also the author of the novel *Land of Love and Drowning*, which won the 2014 Flaherty-Dunnan First Novel Award from the Center for Fiction, the Phillis Wheatley Award for Pan-African Literature, and the American Academy of Arts and Letters Rosenthal Family Foundation Award, and was listed by NPR as one of the Best Books of 2014. *Land of Love and Drowning* was also a finalist for the Orion Award in Environmental Literature and the

about the authors

Hurston-Wright Legacy Award. Tiphanie is the author of a collection of stories, *How to Escape from a Leper Colony*, which won her a listing as one of the National Book Foundation's 5 Under 35. Her writing has also won the Bocas Award for Caribbean Fiction, the Boston Review Prize in Fiction, a Rona Jaffe Foundation Writers Award, a Pushcart Prize, a Fulbright Scholarship, and an Academy of American Poets Prize. She has been listed by the *Boston Globe* as one of the sixteen cultural figures to watch out for, and her writing has been published in the *New York Times, Best African American Fiction, The Wall Street Journal, American Short Fiction*, and other places. Tiphanie is from the Virgin Islands and is an associate professor in the MFA program at the New School in New York City, where she is the 2015 recipient of the Distinguished Teaching Award. She lives in New Rochelle, New York, with her husband, teacher and photographer Moses Djeli, and their three children.

Lightning Source UK Ltd.
Milton Keynes UK
UKOW02f1234130417
299034UK00002B/83/P